Welcome to Necropolis #1: Dark Tomorrow

K.L. Miller

Copyright © 2014 K.L. Miller

All rights reserved.

ISBN: 0692251170
ISBN-13: 978-0692251171

DEDICATION

This is dedicated to God and Lauren Hairston; they know why.

CONTENTS

ACKNOWLEDGMENTS

I want to thank Spark Schmitt for the outstanding cover art and deep wisdom; everyone should have an Artist for a good friend!

PROLOGUE: HUMAN SHADOWS

The house smelled and sounded like Sunday-after-Church Dinner in a Southern Black Home; the tall, rakishly handsome young black man sucked the last remnants of his wife's outstanding fried chicken from his fingertips before leaning away from the dinner table and rubbing his satiated, slightly bulging belly. He sat back with a contented sigh and waited; several seconds later the nicotine urge gripped his jaw muscles, followed closely by the need for a hit from a blunt. Another sigh, this one bloated with *Oh Well*, eased its way from his chest; a hand reached around his left, removing the dinner plate and its ravaged chicken bones. Caden 'Keys' Grace felt his smile tugging at his lips; he loved his wife Camille's rich, wheat colored skin... especially when she smelled... delicious.

"Got room for pecan pie?" Keys raised one eyebrow and started to speak; for a moment he wondered if the growing nicotine fit caused his thoughts to darken. Then he heard it: a deep, insidiously mad Joker-like chuckle rolling across vast, desolate roads cloaked by a moonless, cloud covered night sky. It always happened when looming Work Stress crept into his reality... along with a nagging itch to chill with a not-so-old friend, one Silas Alexander Quick. Tomorrow promised plenty of bullshit at the place they once worked together.

"Save me some for lata, boo." Keys retrieved his half-empty pack of cigarettes from a thigh-pocket on his jeans and a lighter from its counterpart on his right; before he pulled a cigarette from its partially crumpled container his eyes locked on the lighter: a black Bic lighter, a signature of his friend and sometimes running mate, Silas. Before his memories swamped him, drowning out a good end to a good day, Keys lit up and took a long, slow pull from the menthol cigarette; normally he'd spew the smoke from the corner of his mouth. This time he French inhaled, drawing exhaled smoke into his nostrils; then he dragon exhaled, forcing the smoke from his nostrils and mouth. The overall effect shrouded him in deep thought, something his wife noticed quickly even though she could only see the back of his wavy-haired head.

"Baby... what's wrong?"

"Thinkin' 'bout Quick; his Ol' Lady passed; haven't heard from 'im." Keys took another hit from his cigarette, placing his smart phone on the kitchen table haphazardly.

He was searching his Facebook application for any recent activity by his friend when he paused, slightly confused. He quickly searched his pockets, erasing his confusion when he realized he'd returned both cigarettes and lighter to their respective pockets. From the living room he heard his eldest son cheer loudly after scoring a touchdown; the rough-play argument from his youngest tugged a smile on his goatee framed lips.

"Told you that New Orleans D can't stop shit!!!" bragged his eldest son.

"Fuck you!!" spat his youngest child; Keys chuckled, knowing what would come next and silently taking notice of the strange coincidence; Silas was a survivor of the great tragedy known as Hurricane Katrina, and even though born in Virginia, considered the Big Easy **HOME**.

"**Watch your mouth... BOTH of you!!** Go see him." Keys cocked his head, staring into his wife's hazel eyes as his soft, gruff chuckle faded; his smile saddened slightly, teetering towards his all too familiar savvy Street Player as he replied.

"Can't just drop by; not a good idea, boo." He groaned softly as she massaged his shoulders. She never said anything else, but he knew her well enough to understand: she'd nag him with subtle hints until he made the effort to check up on his friend and **not** just by following him online. If he didn't go see him she'd give him shit about it until either an argument ensued or he gave in and paid him a visit.

* * * *

Trust me... trust him!

Making a mental note to thank Keys' Ol' Lady Properly, I gratefully broke up a **FAT** bud of Midnight Bliss. I'd wondered if Keys got a call from Melodie, but until his Thoughts drifted towards his Ol' Lady, I didn't know what dragged him from his usual safe perch at home. Keys is notoriously bad about calling *or* visiting anyone unless there was Biz to conduct; that's one of the main reasons I like him. He reminds me of most of the people I know/knew back Home... a familiar Presence in unfamiliar waters.

"You really wanna go to da club tonight, brah? **REALLY** not feelin' the drama." I frowned as I scrutinized the weed pile for anything that would ruin the smoke; there **were** no seeds or stems in the powerful marijuana, but protocol demanded I make the effort.

"Well... let's slip by the old place; think Jill's working." Which meant Melodie would hear that I'm back in town, but not for several days. It gave me a chance to return to old stomping grounds, and for a brief moment I wondered if the managers I'd bumped heads with were still there. Thoughts of revenge against Carl flashed white-hot, yet lack even the memory of truly heated Hatred; I should be grateful, but considering how

I worked **very** hard to eliminate Hate from my emotional pile, I could just manage a darkly amused inner chuckle, nowhere near enough to ruin a good Blunt Session.

"Blaze first; don't wanna set foot in that hell hole sober," I growled. *Sober there are no Excuses* and there was just enough Hate within my Soul that I wasn't comfortable entering a place filled with so much unfinished Street Biz. Keys dumped the cigarillo's guts into the trashcan I provided; I prefer smoking marijuana from glass pipes or a hookah, but Street Protocol requires blunts among African American weed heads.

"I know that's right!" We started to burn the blunt and shoot shit about Life and the people we know; I was listening, but more intent on enjoying the rare opportunity to hang with someone I consider a friend. Keys always rolls tight blunts and this one was no exception; we were halfway through the session when I felt the need for Street Tunes.

I muttered, "Tunes," and rose; before I actually stepped towards my bedroom I Sensed his Thoughts drifting on his high. They floated over a familiar Image: my deceased lover Jeanie, and I was tremendously grateful for being stoned; it prevented my instinctive urge to Burn her memory from my friend's mind forever. He knew how much I truly love her, and feared I wouldn't recover from the nightmare that was her death. He knew ***NOTHING*** of the truth behind her death, and for that I am eternally grateful.

Necropolis hasn't been friendly; since the day I arrived, shell-shocked from Hurricane Katrina's devastation of my beloved home New Orleans, the city and most of its inhabitants have done their damn level best to utterly obliterate everything I worked so hard to become. Were it not for Keys and Jeanie and several others I'm almost certain I'd be dead by my own hand; they helped me stay grounded... remain **HUMAN**... when everyone else seemed determined to hammer all traces of Big Easy and Humanity from my Mind and Soul, and force me to behave as **they** believed a nice-looking, disturbingly polite and intensely intelligent Black Guy *should*: Happy House Nigga hiding homosexuality by being intelligent and polite. Even marijuana has taken on a different meaning; back in the Big Easy it was the Vice I accepted as part of the shadow community known as Big Easy Cooks. Now it's a crutch I lean on: chemical happiness inhaled to keep myself from snapping and ripping off heads just because some fuckhead decided to poke the bear with a short, sharp stick, believing a verbal apology made everything fine-and-dandy.

I Felt the Moment before Keys said anything: time to hit the streets. Right then the song changed, and a broad, cruel smile spread through my body: Tech N9ne - Harvey Dent; fitting song since there are few alive who like the strange duality represented by my existence. Most are comfortable with the false image they demand: a nice guy they can screw over and insult with perfect Southern Genteel slickness... the nice guy who'll smile and laugh and let them continue to abuse and denigrate him at every turn; the savage, ruthless, utterly heartless bastard forged in the Sprawl... the unusual, disturbingly twisted Soul who survived the Big Easy Shadows and Mother Nature's seething wrath... **that** they want no part of... now or ever. They can't see anything worthwhile in that person; they only see darkness and hellfire's conflagration destroying a toy they like playing with, and within this Image... there is only Fear.

Jeanie saw something within that chaos, and I consider her someone sent by God. Because of her I knew Love when all I had was depression and stress; because of her I know the pain of loss. Keys, he recognizes the Street Warrior behind this intelligent face. He's had his wars and done his Dirt; like me he's trying to stay legit when bills and Life keep their pressure up, stressing the nerves beyond snapping. Melodie was the first female to *attempt* to reach the human being curled up inside my Soul, surrounded by razorblade armor. They remind me that not everyone in Necropolis is worthless; there are good people here. They tend to be hidden, and that's nothing less than Survival Instinct.

"A yo... ready?"

"Yeah...; let's go, Keys." I checked my pockets for my wallet and keys and grabbed my lighter. Before I checked the lock on my front door I alerted the guardian spirits and House Gnomes to my exodus; I didn't rely on ADT or some other outside security agency to protect the meager things within my house. I relied on the power God granted me: my Psionic ability. It's a better deal in my opinion; everything secured I stepped into the Necropolis night, instantly swamped by the smells of oak and maple and pine, Winter's warning breath and that pervasive Sense of Normalcy: Fear, desperation and stupidity roam the Streets.

* * * *

Baked, smellin' good... *and sporting Street Armor:* ***White Tee and black Rosary***; we stopped by Gary's Mart where only two skanked-out Hoes wandered the aisles. They weren't even worth the time to dismiss them, so I made sure to avoid eye contact; this was easily done since my high was rapidly mutating into cruel, rancid evil. I Listened to the generally bitchy, poorly schooled tone of the excessively loud standard Hood Rat conversation they spew, but ignored the nick-names-heavy blather's details. Keys ran into one of his Partnas who popped in for gas and got wind of a house party in one of Necropolis' housing developments; he'll hit that after dropping me by my doss most likely. I'm not too wiz with rubbin' elbows with Loud-Mouth Ballers and I *really* don't want a Sausage Party either. We made our way out into the parking lot... where I Felt Keys thinking a Name; the Memories it brings flood my Mind as I prepared for the onslaught from his lips.

"You think about Jeanie much?"

"Try not to; hurts too much." We got inside his donk and buckled up; I checked the Minds outside of our vehicle, Searching for hidden patrol cars with Assassins looking for easy prey.

"Gotta get out there yo; find somethin' easy and do you." For an instant Melodie's face flashed across his Mind; he wiped it away, dismissing her as an option because he thinks she cares too much for me. He had no idea how right he was.

"Easier if I were back Home ya 'eard me? Hit da strip clubs... stroll down Bourbon... scare somethin' up." Looking outside I imagined Cocaine Corner's rancid neon Peace/Bliss while ignoring the sterilized terror that is my current reality. I missed the sights and sounds of the Big Easy... the flavors and ghosts lurking in the French Quarter... the wildly beautiful quiet chaos of the Faubourg Marigny... the peaceful swamp serenade underpinning the boisterous Bywater; the constant dead-drone Necropolis silence is maddening, always feeling as if it is nibbling steadily at what little sanity I retain while drooling vile, fetid Fear upon whatever happens to be nearby. "Got blunt?"

"**HOW** can you still smoke?"

"That's for later; I'm good for now." I pulled a black wood one-hitter from a concealed pocket within my denim jacket and packed the ceramic bat; satisfied with my efforts I sparked up. The butt end of the bat looked like a normal cigarette, completing the illusion of Normalcy; only someone who knows me would spot the sleight-of-hand: ***I don't smoke cigarettes!!!*** I re-up my high more, once more thinking about how marijuana has become a true What-Me-Worry instead of a piece of candy one treats himself to every now and again.

"Cool; one more thing about Jeanie and I'm done. Do you still love her?" I passed him the bat while I held the pungent smoke for the Stoner required fourteen seconds; after a quick inhale-then-hold I breathed out the smoke, coughed out the dregs still lingering in my lungs and answered once the coughing fit subsided and my High, re-energized, settled behind my eyes.

"Gave my Word: Beyond Eternal, **I will *always* Love her.**" Keys smiled, his gold teeth catching one of the few white street lights and adding even more devil-may-care to his dashing O.G. personality.

"Then *fuck* some other broad yo; get that shit outta ya system before it turns you into a hoarder hermit or sum shit; *I MISS my Nigga.*" I wasn't surprised by the honesty in his tone; in fact... I basked in the Trust he showed, smiling honestly and broadly as I replied.

"Not like your Ol' Lady's gonna let you out!" I joked.

"She will if its **you**; YOU'RE THE GOOD GUY!!!" We laughed at the lie as we rolled through the slow, creeping death that passes for Night in Necropolis.

* * * *

Cook's Law: ***NEVER hang out where you WORK or used to Work!!!***

Normal people enter an establishment through the front door; Keys is a Regular, known and, if you take the Female attention his presence garners superficially, loved. Before entering I Focused my Thoughts inward, calming the growing evil threatening to fill my face with nothing less than Big Easy Hard Heart... or worse: Runner-on-Biz; while it is true I was there on Personal Biz there wasn't a present need to have a Mean Mug or Screw Face plastered over my grill, much less for the cold, ruthlessly emotionless mask I preferred when *Working*. We sauntered silently inside and I immediately scanned the crowd, running an internal IFF - Identify Friend or Foe; the hostess was cleaning a nearby table when she spotted us. She smiled and went through the Greeting routine... until she **really** looked at me. She widened her smile once she recognized me, but didn't give me a hug; fair enough, since the guy she's cheating on her boyfriend with was plastered in a corner with a few of his friends. Keys got a full hug naturally; standing six-five he bent over to receive his Street-Love, his broad smile and smooth baritone voice rolled casually as she squealed her pleasure. She remembered much, like I'm **never** there in Civies unless there's Biz to conduct, and didn't give me more than a casual second glance while heading into the kitchen area to **warn** everyone of my presence; I continued scanning the crowd more from habit than any real reason: Busy Weekend on the Streets, complete with Families grabbing a bite before cloistering themselves within Houses and Homes greeted my casually narrowed gaze. I recognized a few Players and Regulars, nodding respectfully as my High slowly ground into black aggravation.

No one worthy; wrong Hunting Grounds... We lingered only long enough to verify this, each of us taking a shot and Keys making his usual schmooze-rounds. The general manager swung through the dining area, glancing nervously at me several times; I ignored them, Focusing my Thoughts on the hungry Spirit lurking in the Kitchen. Seems no one bothered to keep up its feeding of rib-eye blood; that will cost them, and while I don't show it, there is a salivating, cruel Justice within my Thoughts at this notion. Almost on cue I heard someone I recognized swear loudly... followed by Ol' Man Martin's boisterous barking laugh and, "The Curse of Quick!!"

"He's out there; **HUSH!!!**" I allowed myself a smug smile as I Felt **FEAR** grip those I cannot see.

* * * *

It wasn't long before it was time to roll out; fortunately we didn't start drama, so there's no Tale to tell Melodie except for my presence, disappearance, and the disturbance in the Back of the House just before Martin mentioned my name. As I turned, stuffing my wallet into my back pocket my gaze slid towards the door... where a group of former high school classmates gathered. I recognized a few faces... but some of those faces are worthy of real Notice.

Shit...; KAREN!!

I've known her since grade school... and ***still*** remember the St. Valentine's Day card I wrote for her, but never gave her. Cowardly action that, and yet I still Remember it and the ravishing beauty who never received that boyhood innocent gesture; as I Recalled the shameful Memory an ancient Memory-Voice in my Head roars softly, reminding me of its presence... and its determination to keep me from approaching her. It kept saying I wasn't good enough or ready for her; it **terrified** me: the Powerful Fear that gripped me then. Now?

Now I *leaned* on my alcohol/marijuana Buzz; I was terrified of her Seeing/seeing me in what **I** consider my normal appearance...

She's looking... at us!

Yeah... and by all that is Holy... ***she's smiling!!!***

She has no Idea...; utter Darkness... and complete Truth. I stifled the shudder as I shook off enough Buzz to appear Necropolis Normal to her eyes.

She should not Witness...

"QUICK!!!" I flicked my eyes to the voice and cursed silently; I chided myself for my inattention, though it was easily understood.

She is a proverbial Light Skinned **GODDESS!!!** Svelte... gorgeous... heap the gracious Words on her; Sexy is at the **bottom...** FUCKIN' Foundation!!! Some Females wear tight jeans or slacks and it becomes apparent the garments make the body's shape; her **body** made the sweet, seductive, sweeping lines and the clothes were just there. Stylish... but they did not make her stylish; indeed... they were subjugated by her natural, radiant beauty and overpowering sexuality. I should be drooling over the mere **THOUGHT** of a roll in the hay... even something as seemingly innocent as flirtatious innuendo; instead...

Toss and Toss Aside; Next. Seriously... as much as I'd like a romp with her...

We need Pain. We Need Passion.

WE HUNGER!!!

I accepted the hug graciously but kept a Death-grip on my Mind-fragged fueled Lust and the Dark Thoughts of the Master; I caught a glimpse of the large engagement ring she flashed and know enough about the wagging tongues in town to *help* her when someone blabbed about the so-called Other Guy they saw her hugging in what *they* perceive as more-than-friends. Take Ol' Man Martin, who'd made his way from the Kitchen when he heard I was present; I Felt his broad grin the instant his eyes landed on me. He would ask Keys later about the light-skinned honey holding me tightly, and **that** conversation would somehow find its way around, in some twisted manner and completely filled with Lies and bullshit, until Melodie heard... accidentally of course. Welcome to Necropolis.

"Hello, Silas." *Damn...*

"Good evening Miss Karen; how have you been?" The switch was so sudden I Felt Keys react. I bowed formally, struggling to keep my features pleasant and inviting. She smiled and I found myself wishing I wasn't high and working on a good tequila drunk; Karen's the kind of Woman who, just with a look, makes a Male pull himself upright and hold himself with proper composure. I could see her in a formal dress with a glass of wine or champagne, but the *concept* of her tipsy seemed appalling. From grade school... throughout high school... she was and will always be a Lady. In truth... and as Defined by one of the Clan Cursed; that was disturbing, since **every** Lady known to the Clan Cursed has known Darkness, Pain and Suffering. My Hunger swung its ebony gaze towards her Soul; before I could glimpse anything I yanked back on the instinctive urge to pry into her Thoughts... **MIND RAPE** her for the dark Thoughts this Definition demanded be within her Mind and Soul.

I chatted with both women, discovering that they were early arrivals, expecting more African American former classmates shortly. I was grateful when the others arrived; it gave me time to order another shot of 1800, steady my nerves and catch up with Martin. While I didn't expect to hear anything unexpected, I never pass up the opportunity to solidify relations with a good Contact; Biz... even when relaxing: an old Sprawl Axiom. It is better stated thusly:

Biz... NEVER Personal chummer...

* * * *

Angie felt herself adjust her features; her gaze wanted to linger on Silas as he ***pimp-strolls*** towards the impromptu Reunion but she knew well the gossip waiting for her should she reveal just how well she knows the enigmatic black man. Someone behind her remarks how fake his movements appear; she didn't reply, eyes focused just beyond his Street hardened gaze and the smooth, casual Mask he wore. Outwardly he was just another Local enjoying a night out.

Yet within her Mind: she Saw a ghostly Female standing just behind him and to his right hand side. The Mask he wore faded away, revealing the troubled visage of a Young Black Man struggling with inner demons and doubt. Sadness and turmoil plagued her Thoughts as she blinked, the conflicting Images somehow... perfectly complimentary on his intelligent, gentle features.

He Misses his Love... and it's driving him into that Prison.

She avoided Thinking about the cruel Darkness simmering behind his obviously intoxicated-but-Maintaining smile; she chuckled at his dashing flourish with his black fedora, but her Heart beat heavily. Movement drew her attention back to her beautiful daughter, a Student of **Lord** Silas Quick, the Man she knows lies carefully tucked away within the flesh, hidden by faint yet visceral Darkness and Shadow.

Hiding in Plain Site: The Truth of Klowns he said.

* * * *

* * * *

"Nothin' back there?" Keys grinned, raising one eyebrow; he's thinking about Karen and my sudden transformation from Hood Nigga to Proper Gentleman. The only other Female he knows I do that with is Jeanie; he won't ask, but he **will** poke and prod.

"*NOT WITHOUT DRAMA*," I sighed heavily; chuckling, I continued. "Keys... I'm In a Mood. That's dat Bondage stuff."

"**SO?** Same thing Bo: nothin' back there? Those girls back there **all** read your stuff, right? You **really** gotta work dat shit." I raised one eyebrow and stared at Keys as a smirking smile flit around my lips rapidly.

"What: Erotica to the MILFs in Necropolis - the Real Tales?" Being a Dirty Little Secret isn't new to me, but it is a Sensation I loath greatly; I didn't like it when Jeanie and I first began our relationship (she Lurked on the web page where I posted my Tales) and I despised having secret fans of my writing. I understood the concept well; I Lurked the darker Net Shadows when the Internet was just beginning its pervasive march into Society. And while they *are* fans, they would not **admit** to it in front of their peers, much less in a Court of Law; this fucked-up dichotomy always intrigued me... and always nags at the part of me that doesn't give an almighty **flyin'** fuck... so long as people Live within the Light of Who and What They Are.

"Shit's pretty fuckin' real as-is; kinda hard to believe you just sit in your room and think that shit up, Bo. *And I hear tell you got more than one at the new WORK huntin' you Down!!!*"

"Now **how** the fuck do you..." I laughed, stopping myself from asking the obvious question; Keys knows everyone... **and nothing at all: Code of the Street Samurai.** Of course, he let slip that **he** reads my works, as does his Ol' Lady; she explains his occasional appearance on my Facebook site as I'm fairly sure he doesn't spend any real time lurking online and has no real interest in my erotic Tales. And during those quiet moments when my name happens to come up, Keys gains insights not only into his Ol' Lady, but those she knows. He learned a long time ago: **LISTENING** to the Winds is one of the keys to survival... pardon the pun.

"Chris; he told me. We should swing by his place." It isn't a complete lie, and his words reminded me of something I've been neglecting: **Pack**.

"Yeah... been a minute since I've seen Fam; he's been workin' his ass off."

"Not to mention a wife and three kids!! Think he'll appreciate a good buzz!"

"True dat-dat; gonna hit 'im up first so his Ol' Lady don't freak out?" Keys' smart phone beeped: biz from the way his eyes momentarily lost their pleasant sheen; Money don't wait and from the instant he set foot outside his house I was expecting someone to hit him up. Still, he adhered to the Man Code: Friends First; he fired off a quick text message before roaring off into the Necropolis night. We hit the side streets, dipping through the shadow drenched streets with bass pushing out chests and pumping the blood. I almost let myself forget the tumultuous memories and the stress; then I spotted a police cruiser's spotlight flipping through a trailer park. The Streets are never quiet for very long; get caught slippin' and you'll find yourself behind bars or face down leaking like a sieve.

So I Focused my Thoughts; I Sensed the Minds tucked away in houses and homes... Families and lone Souls and every category of Humanity. This is the Necropolis no one wants known, the side of the city everyone whispers about and texts their BFF about; this is the seedy and comfortable, the pristine Normalcy and the filthy Dirt: Business as usual in Your City, USA.

"Probably lookin' for kids havin' a party; college is out."

"True dat-dat," I breathed; it reminded me of my two Charges: L.J. and Marcus. They should be coming home for the holidays; this is their city now. I have other things filling my time. We crept by the ongoing search and were well on our way when I Sensed the chaos as the Assassins raided the gathering: Life in the Shadows of the Streets. Two trailers over an old man poked his head out of his front window, his ears filled with the police scanner's static heavy squawk giving the blow-by-blow details he's observing... and I'm not surprised that Fear and sadistic glee war within his Thoughts.

L.J. - FAMILY TIES

"How was your first semester at college, son?"

"Not bad, Dad; made a few friends... even managed to pass most of my classes with Bs."

"Keep up the good work, I'm proud of you."

L.J. smiled; things between them seemed better, though the somewhat slender young man placed that to being apart from each other. Of course, he also considered the shift in his fashion style; he no longer went for a fusion of Country-Boy Hip-Hop and complete mismatched geek. Stylish sneakers and loose-fitting denim started a climb towards College Kid; the Winter coat sported college colors with the name emblazoned across his shoulders. L.J. thought he looked rather... Normal, and would often check his appearance in the full-length door mirror tacked to the back of his dorm room door, confirming the transition he often considered part of Growing Up. As he stood before his father L.J. knew the change was rudely obvious; even L.J.'s ever-present baseball cap, the brim covering the back of his neck as always, draped the young man in Normalcy. He swiped it off with one hand and used the free hand to adjust his close cropped black locks; this seemed to remind his father of the young man who bummed around Necropolis. Smiling, the elder Ellis clasped his son's hand firmly.

"Seen Marcus yet?"

"He's not coming home; he got a job working in a kitchen and is staying with someone. I figure it's his new girlfriend he won't tell me about." *Besides: if I need him all I've gotta do is Reach Out.*

"Speaking of girlfriends..." L.J. lowered his head, his smile fading with ominous, agonizing slowness despite his feeble attempt to morph it into a Player's grin.

"I haven't seen Dominique since we parted ways for college." He lifted his head, a cocky smirk now etched on his lips. "And I wasn't exactly **looking** to replace her with anyone." His father laughed and L.J. chuckled softly; his dad seemed genuinely pleased with his only child and for a moment L.J. simply basked in the sensation. Then concern filled his father's worn, slightly weathered face.

"You gonna go back to work during your vacation?" His father dropped L.J.'s hand naturally, but his son saw the turmoil churning behind those warm brown eyes. L.J. softened his smirk before answering.

"He hasn't called; haven't heard from Silas Quick in a while now." His father nodded silently. L.J. used to drive clients for the enigmatic black man, and it was rumored the Passengers went to his secret pleasure palace known locally as Darkhaven Manor. Miles Ellis inhaled suddenly and his features shifted as he quickly changed subjects; L.J. took notice of the difference, his right eyebrow twitching upwards slightly.

"Hungry? I've got a gift card burnin' a hole in my pocket." L.J. almost said no. Then he caught a glimpse of the restaurant's name as his father waved the plastic card and *almost* strayed within one stray thought of *definitely NOT*; L.J. blinked and felt his right eye twitch again. At that instant a soft buzzing sensation scratched the nape of his neck.

"Sure; lemme get cleaned up first." *Not to mention Prepare; Lord Quick's curse on that place is probably still there.* "And you're driving!"

"Sounds good t' me!! Just don't take all day; I ain't eat lunch!!" L.J. half strode, half bounced up the stairs as he headed for the bathroom. He washed his face and rinsed his mouth; without any real Thought he formed an intricate series of hand motions, sighing with satisfaction as the buzzing in his neck faded into a calm, whispering wind over a deep blue lake.

* * * *

The place Feels foul... tainted. L.J. chatted with his father easily; he never liked sticking to local gossip and news while in high school, but it served a twisted purpose now as they sipped their drinks and allowed their meals to cool slightly. L.J. tried ignoring the loud group of high school teenagers and children running wild while their parents screamed at them to behave or ignored them completely. It was difficult, but not because he lacked patience; Psionic energy was everywhere. He labored when breathing its viscous, moist essence; it overloaded his nerves as electricity ate at neurons. His muscles flexed spasmodically and L.J. felt his emotions dart about with wide-eyed panic, each one desperate to know the source of their inexplicable aggravation.

And **LUST**; L.J. drank two full glasses of water in a vain attempt to wash down that emotion's muddy Feel. Frustration forced him to rely on skills learned years past, and as he continued to catch up on random things with his father the wiry eighteen year old placed both elbows on the table and folded his hand over and over again, intricately interlacing his strong, skeletal fingers over and over again until the proper *kuji-in* were performed and the Power within him formed the Psionic Walls. Yet even then... before those Walls formed around his Thoughts... L.J. Felt an ancient, immensely powerful Presence. It turned invisible eyes towards him, and L.J. was astonished by the sensation that those large orbs were partially closed, as if the infinitely cruel, beyond ancient... **thing...** slept through a familiar noise.

"Some things never change."

"Not in this town, son. I'm glad we had this chance; can't remember the last meal we had together." L.J. spotted their server as his Walls solidified; he kept his Snape-like features placidly pleased as Lust remained the only recognizable Sensation. *It's **EVERYWHERE** in this place!!!* The thing snorted/snored an irritated growl, and L.J. felt as if it had just judged him: young and foolish.

"How about you Dad? You're still single..." L.J. silently signaled his father; Miles turned and flashed his best smile for the well built honey skinned server. L.J. ignored his father's gaze lingering on cleavage by staring at the steak on his plate; it doesn't look particularly appetizing, but the effort helped mask the Lust radiating from the server... and the sensation that she is ***consciously*** throttling it up and down. *It's like being on a beach and looking out at a tsunami you just **KNOW** hides a Rouge Wave in its fury.*

"And I'm gonna **stay** single; women 'round here can't keep their mouths shut or stay outta someone's business." Miles leaned forward and dropped his voice conspiratorially, and the elder Ellis even glanced over his shoulder to see if their server was safely out of hearing range before speaking.

"You still runnin' the Streets?"

"No need; made supervisor at the factory!!" Miles said, leaning back and smiling proudly.

Not that you like it. L.J. congratulated his father, clamping down on the savage, ruthless, primal Rage filtering into his Thoughts. Yet as the dinner progressed the dark haired L.J. noticed something: there was no controlling Presence. One of the managers had Sex-on-the-Brain, making it painfully easy to pierce his Wall of Thoughts; though L.J. had no *reason* to enter his mind, he wasn't surprised by his skill at doing so. Nor was he overly concerned when he Felt a poltergeist's attention fixing on his physical form. He prepared to do combat within the Thoughtscape while trying to chew a piece of his tough steak. He began by interlacing his fingers, leaving only the thumb tips touching; as he Sensed Time slow he Heard the poltergeist hiss/chitter and scurry away. It snapped at the manager before retreating into the kitchen, and the ancient entity watched... with quiet approval; as L.J.'s index fingers moved one name popped into his Mind, bringing with it raw Darkfyre, and the answer. Where he Sensed a void... where he Sensed a controlling Mind was needed... there was the inhumanly unholy and impossibly calm and Focused presence he knew as his former Teacher: Lord Silas Quick, Master of Darkhaven Manor.

* * * *

"Sex is the easiest way to enter the Human Mind because *everyone* Thinks about Sex at least once in their Life."

L.J. smiled quietly as he watch the familiar buildings whiz by; they drove home accompanied by the engine's smooth drone and the illusory silence of Thoughts.

*Now I know Why the Old Man found working there so aggravating; musta took everything he **had** to stay **OUT** of the Minds in that place. Never imagined so many horny dumb-asses could fit inside one building, let alone **work** together; half expected to see Jeanie...*

"You should call her." His father's voice didn't shatter his concentration; it was an expected thing and L.J. reacted with velvet smoothness.

"Who: Dom?"

"Of course; I'm sure she'd like to hear from you... oh shit."

L.J. saw the flashing blue lights; still on edge from his restaurant experience he adjusted his posture by sinking into the seat a bit and cleared his Mind, readying himself for whatever happened.

"Think they got robbed again?" L.J. asked quietly.

"Don't doubt it; that place's been hit more times this year... and there's been a string of robberies recently. We've even had two bank robberies!!" Miles Ellis went from proud father to seasoned Creature of the Night swiftly and smoothly; his upright and alert posture became a familiar shadow-slump and his right hand fell from the steering wheel onto the floor-mounted gear shifter. L.J. wanted to smile when his father's arm wiggled; their car was an automatic, not the stick-shift he'd sold before L.J. went to college.

"They caught those guys; I remember hearing about it on the news."

"Yeah... but I'll bet you didn't hear that they never recovered the **money!!**"

"Actually, the news said they'd recovered it."

"Lie; word I get is they haven't recovered one **dime** from ***any*** of the robberies from the past two months. I figure there's a dirty cop stashin' the money away before ratting out the robbers."

L.J. chuckled dismissively. Even so, as they crept past the scene of the crime he entered a police woman's mind, crashing through her tightly focused Thoughts with enough Force to physically move the slender African American and cause her to stumble. L.J. tore through her Mind, quickly discarding Thoughts he deemed useless until he came across one name.

Strange; she's thinking about Lord Quick. The cops can't ***really*** *be so... wait: I forgot where I am. The stranger the details the more likely they are to look for a* *scapegoat... and he makes a damned good one.* As he pulled out of her Mind and the car continued on, L.J. saw the female officer shake her head, clearly disoriented. He faced forward, oddly calm and never thinking about the damage his Intrusion may have left.

* * * *

The trip now passed in complete silence; L.J. and his father screwed their faces in tight concentration as orange neon and stark white halogen splashed over houses, the obligatory church and parked vehicles. L.J. knew his father was driving around instead of heading straight home, but he didn't mind; something very powerful stalked the Night and its stealthy movements left tell-tale signs... *if you knew where to look and possessed the ability to See.* L.J. was so Focused that he nearly missed the familiar surroundings of his neighborhood.

"Looks like your employer's here." L.J. didn't reply as the car slowly crept towards his home; *that's not the Old Man... that's Meanstreak.* The simplistic Audi A6 was definitely out of place in the neighborhood. L.J. recognized the familiar Thoughts Consolidated Deep Space midnight black, and razor's edge chrome accents the Master of Chains preferred when he required mortal transportation betrayed the identity of the male-shaped shadow seated behind the steering wheel. They drove past the parked A6 and L.J. reached out with a single, focused Thought.

Whatever's roaming around, it ain't Meanstreak.

"Gonna be gone for a while?" His father killed the engine without fanfare, but his words blatantly trumpeted gruff concern and worry rang clarion.

"Not likely Dad; I'll be inside shortly. Just gonna find out what he wants real fast."

L.J. stepped into the chilled night air as if his belly were full, groaning with effort as he stretched his back and arms; few would recognize such movements as tactical proficiency, for L.J.'s eyes darted over every nearby shadow during his stretching. Nor would anyone outside of certain circles understand the intricate patterns he created with his hands; with sublime subtlety he performed several complex hand gestures, weaving together complex and powerful Psionic energies. In the twenty seconds it took for the wiry, narrow-eyed college freshman to walk to the edge of his front yard, L.J. successfully secured his home from all but the most powerful Psionic attacks and formed several Constructs tasked with monitoring a two block radius; **he also** reached out to the local stray cat and dogs, touching their Minds gently. Only when satisfied that there was no immediate threat did L.J. slide inside the non-reflective black sedan. A curiously devious smile played across his lips as he closed the passenger side door; a stray cat froze, alerted by the shifting light from a window. *Nosy Mrs. Helen; some things never change.*

"Your Senses are sharper than before; you will need that." There were few sounds capable of terrifying L.J.; Meanstreak's inhumanly emotionless, hollow voice never failed to inspire naked fear. L.J. was momentarily worried when he realized the hooded figure seated in the driver's seat had no arms; the moment passed with the soft clink of metallic chains and L.J. turned his attention to the dashboard display, purposefully ignoring the urge to look for the source of the rattling chains.

"Hello to you too, Killer; what brings you by?"

"You have need of a vehicle while you are here; I am here to deliver it."

"Is that it?"

"Indeed; I have other matters to attend to, and **you** have a Life to Live, Human."

"I expected... more." L.J. looked around the vehicle's interior haphazardly, waiting for the shadow on his left to continue.

"And more you will receive, though not from me. Beneath your seat are Lord Quick's final instructions... and a Gift."

"What about Marcus?"

"My former Charge walks a different Path, though your connection is still there." The hooded figure lowered his head slightly before continuing. "You will need each other... and you will both have need of the White Witch; there are things happening within this city that require the Skills you've all learned... yet only **you** have expanded upon." With his last ominous words Meanstreak the Master of Chains melted into the black seat; one link from his ever-present chains appeared briefly and touched the keys left in the ignition. L.J. stared at the d-link it kissed before vanishing, wondering what meaning lay in its action. He reached beneath his seat and pulled a small black box from a space he knew was too small for the black wood box. Inside there was note written on parchment; it covered a hematite rosary, similar to the one favored by Lord Quick.

*The thing **oozes** Power!!!* He glanced at the note, a full two words long: **Welcome Home.** He hesitated briefly before placing the rosary over his head; when he tucked it next to his flesh he felt it drain away negative energy, cooling well beyond hematite's normal tendency to do so when placed against the flesh. *I'll examine it later; right now...* he removed the keys from the ignition and exited the A6. He wasn't surprised when it locked down the instant he closed the door, nor was he stunned by the Psionic energy he Sensed from the seemingly dormant vehicle. All Thoughts Consolidated vehicles possessed some artifacts, but this vehicle seemed almost alive.

Things are definitely heating up in Necropolis. He flicked his eyes over the shadows, smiling as their natural darkness peeled away.

MARCUS - DOWN THE COVERED PATH

The kitchen breathes easier at the end of the night, even at the end of the semester. The loudest noises are the hissing dishwasher, pans and dishes chattering as they find their place on the drying racks, silverware clashing, and the occasional human noises. Non-slip shoes squeak on rapidly drying floors; smart phone speakers strain beneath bass heavy rap or choke/scream out high-frequency club tunes, and barking laughter rattles its way through the dining area as servers blather on and on about upcoming adventures and gossip. In the actual kitchen the sounds of cleaning spike the sanitizer solution bloated air; song lyrics surprised the semi-emptiness with impromptu ad-libs and varying levels of singing/rapping ability. Four bodies occupied the kitchen area: two Line Cooks completed the closing procedures for the line, another tidied up the back prep area, and one dish washer moved rhythmically within the stainless steel dish pit. One Line Cook looked up from his task, a satisfied half-smile firmly set on his lips as his eyes surveyed the clean stainless steel; he turned his steady gaze towards his knife kit and the rapidly drying cutting boards waiting for their placement as a deep voice scrambled from within the chromed dish machine.

"Yo... Mar-Kus!!!"

"Whaddup G-man?"

"Wanna chill wi' the boys tonight? Or's ya Girl got the leash on ya ass again tonight!!!"

"Shut ya mouth!! Spendin' vay-kay with her and her folks up in West Virginia."

"WHAAAAAA?!?!?! Dey know you black?"

Marcus Aurellius Robertson flung the cleaning towel in his hands at Greg "G-man"; though he was definitely a big man the dish wash night supervisor moved with surprising speed, swatting the towel out of the air while dancing to one side.

"They don't care."

"Uh huh... and you know this how?"

"My Ol' Lady..."

"Look here, Pretty Boy," came a high-pitched, nasal voice from the back prep area, "*never* trust a female who tells you shit like that."

"Whitey... like your dumb ass knows what females would do!?!" G-man fired his words around the concrete wall.

"Uh... ***HELLO!!!***" Darrel "Smitty" Smith shook his head; everyone except Marcus laughed at the inside joke. Ralph "Whitey" Whitman is openly gay and *often* takes pot-shots at himself.

"I ain't sayin' ya girl's a bitch... but **I** *know* how bitches are; she'll **say** her parents won't mind but just wait 'til they corner your ass!!" Greg and Darrel started ragging Ralph; Marcus smiled softly before telling everyone to calm down.

"I'ma lounge... put on the Dazzle and Charm and have 'em dancin' t' **my** music!!"

"Maaannnn... Whitey got you cold; you **ARE** a Pretty Boy!!" Marcus grinned, secretly pleased at this assessment.

* * * *

"Keep your eyes open; deer wander into the road frequently."

"Just like back home; your parents **are** expecting a black man..." Marcus felt himself becoming paranoid at the thought of being trapped so far from home, even though he always had a way back: Shadow Walking. Still... that was a last resort, and one he wasn't looking forward to exploiting unless it was absolutely necessary.

"Like I've told you a million times: they don't ***CARE!!!***" Marcus smiled nervously, though he tried concealing his apprehension with a quick kiss on his girlfriend's cheek.

"Now when Dad's parents show up, things might get a bit ugly..." *Great...;* instinct tickled his Thoughts and he secured his Gateway through the Thoughtscape; he frowned briefly at the effort, but dismissed it as rusty inexperience. He seldom used his abilities at college.

"And one more thing: don't let Grandpa Jackson scare you with tales of hangings in the woods. I figure he'll tell one tale in particular... just to scare you."

"Sweet." His girlfriend, Carrie, placed her hand on his thigh; he smiled warmly, though his Thoughts were anything but warm. Each turn and hill fed an insidious, lethargic paranoia; for an instant Marcus considered plugging his headphones into his smart phone and losing himself in Rap. His gaze drifted over the trees, picking out pine and spruce greenery from the bare branches and night-drenched leaves stubbornly refusing Winter's death-kiss. The mini-SUV swung around a left hand bend; as the road changed direction once more he spotted the small bamboo copse. A quiet, wistful sadness haunted his eyes and darkened the lingering happiness of sandy-haired Carrie's affection.

It's been nearly a year... Even with his self-imposed hiatus, he easily Focused his Thoughts until the Thoughtscape's twisted, chaotic beauty bled into and over Reality. As she drove him deeper into the wooded mountains he Saw the familiar red/green/blue/gold of deer and coyote and a small wolf pack; turkey buzzards glowed Life-warm muted red, and a murder of ravens darted for cover as it Sensed his presence. He Followed them for several heartbeats, but stopped once he caught Sight of the Spirit and the large multi-colored uncertainty as a cougar watched him, a doe it stalked and the phantasm.

"Slow down; there's a doe around the next bend." Marcus noticed a familiar rumbling in his words as his enhanced vision filled with more Reality than Thoughtscape images. He felt the vehicle slow as they rounded the curve; Carrie's yelp came as no surprise, but the blue flash drew the attention of that part of him still peering into the Thoughtscape. His physical body relaxed, but his Thoughts hardened visibly, betrayed only by a slight narrowing of his deceptively intelligent brown eyes.

"How did you know?" Carrie asked as the startled doe bounded into the deep night. She blew out her fear; Marcus remained calm... completely unsurprised.

"Mountain roads here... back woods country roads back home; they all have a certain Feel to 'em." He tried to sound confidently cocky... instead of that not quite curious yet ominously hard blend between Street and Soul Hound.

"Oh Gram Hazel's gonna **love** you!! Some say she's a witch." As soon as he heard the word *witch* his Senses shifted; Reality and the Thoughtscape became one and he forced himself to avoid looking over his girlfriend's head... where he knew a Human Mind approached through the Thoughtscape, moving with unearthly speed as it wound its way through the trees.

They have no idea. His Thought Voice growled low, warning the approaching entity with its inhuman sub-vocalization.

I rather LIKE it that way; greetings Hound.

* * * *

The more distant the building from Normal Society, the greater the Darkness; Marcus silently thanked the old witch for her insights into Family habits, though he could not dismiss the firm grip paranoia held over him. *Place reminds me of Darkhaven Manor... and I'm not sure how she knew I was a Hound. I don't remember encountering her before; she was definitely an unknown Scent.*

Thick gnarled oak trees and majestically dark spruce concealed the large white house; through the darkness he spotted part of a guest house/large tool shed. The air held snowfall in its future; his Senses and brief study of the weather patterns before the trip told him it would be a blizzard. He hoped Witch Hazel wouldn't prevent Carrie's father from making the trip and raised one eyebrow, surprised by his thought; he Sensed Lust within Carrie's Home, the familiar emotion thick and pervasive, threatening to overwhelm his control. The wind rustled the trees overhead, the sound barely covering a malevolent Spirit's hideous groan. Marcus narrowed his eyes slightly, Pushing the thing back into the depths of the night with powerful Thought energy; it did not like a black man on what it considered its property. While talismans and spells kept it out of the house proper, only a proper Banishment would purge the land of its presence. Fully capable of such a task, Marcus only sent the thing away with a low, rumbling Thought-growl; he now had no intention of remaining in West Virginia any longer than absolutely necessary, and did not want it following him should he have need to Shadow Walk away.

"You said it was big, hun; this is a mansion!!" He hoped the surprise he added to his voice sounded genuine and nodded inwardly as Carrie beamed with pride.

"Wait 'till you get inside; dad installed a Jacuzzi just before I left!!" He didn't need to see the dazzle in her crisp blue eyes to know she intended on having sex there. In fact, Marcus toyed with the idea of asking L.J. to link their minds during his stay. The front door opened, throwing soft yellow-white light into the dark. Instinctively Marcus pulled himself up to his full six-foot-two; he worked his powerful jaw muscles and cracked his neck first to one side then the other as Lust leapt from the building's yawning portal. Within his Soul he felt an all too familiar Darkness stir, swinging a lazy Awareness towards the form filling the door's opening.

"**Carrie!!!** I'm so glad you made it before the storm hit!! It's all over the news!!! And this must be Marcus!!"

Now I know where the Lust came from, and Why Carrie is such a panther in bed; her mother reeks from her last masturbation session... not more than an hour ago. As introductions were made Marcus quickly set up another Gateway to his dorm room in college; he was sure that a quick exit **would** be needed before the two weeks was over, and wasn't about to risk Witch Hazel closing down the Gateway to his home. *Carrie's moms is sizing me up like a slab of beef; and what's that I smell: a seduction potion? Looks like Witch Hazel forgot to mention a few things.* He forced a warm smile onto his lips as he looked over his shoulder, watching with a predatory narrowing of his eyes as Carrie's mother locked the door with definite purpose.

DOMINIQUE - THE WITCHING HOUR

Dominique Gordon stared at her smart phone. *He won't call; why am I waiting for him to call?*

"Dominique? You have a visitor!" Dominique ran down the stairs, coming to a rapid stop when she didn't see L.J.'s frame standing at the front door beside her mother.

"Hello, Dominique."

"Mr. Edwards..." Surprise cracked her normally smooth, peculiarly seductive deep voice. Any disappointment or concern was swamped by Mr. Edwards' odd attire; he wore an olive trench coat over an eggplant colored dress shirt... and a shimmering amethyst silk tie that sported a harlequin green paisley print. He looked a great deal like Silas, though his face was longer and the features more Joker-like; several shades darker than Silas, his skin always held an ethereal glow, and this time was no different. She often wondered if the face he wore when out in public was his real one.

"Formal; please call me Alexander. I was wondering if we might talk for a bit..."

"What did she do now!" Dominique rolled her eyes and hissed/sighed; Alexander's professional tone would not cool her mother's near-constant aggravation but she was grateful for the attempt.

"She designed a costume for an actress in a play; the design and implementing caught the attention of a client I represent in France. It took some time to track her down..." Dominique stopped listening; she knew Pushing when she Felt it and closed down the part of Mind responsible for hearing. She slid her gaze towards her mother's face, scowling at the disbelief she saw clearly etched on her mother's features.

If you hate me so much why'd you call every week?!?!

"May we use the Kitchen mother?" The dye-job blonde snorted once before snarling a reply... not that Dominique heard her; it wasn't until she saw a ghostly twinkle in Alexander's eye that the tallish college student Willed her hearing back on, just in time to hear her mother gripe about the Time of Day.

Not to be rude, but she *DEFINITELY* needs a dick in her mouth!!

Probably wouldn't help Dominique thought in reply; she smiled at Alexander and ushered him through the living room and into the kitchen. She chose that room because of something Lord Quick often said: **Life happens in the Kitchen**, and she was certain Alexander Charles Edwards', *Ace's*, visit wasn't the lie he'd Pushed into her mother's Thoughts.

Nosy thing too; don't wanna Push too hard. Sound-Illusion it is then. Ask me if I'd like something to drink and turn your ears off while I set up the Babble Wall.

* * * *

Some people are just too nosy for their own damned good; Dom's mother *said* she was going upstairs but the bitch pulled a U-turn the second we were out of sight. Fortunately I came prepared; the instant her daughter spoke my Mundane first name the incantation would activate. In the end all her nosy mother would *remember* is a polite conversation about fashion. What ***really*** makes Mommy-Dearest a sick twat is **why** she's being nosy; she honestly believes her daughter's sold her soul to become something she isn't. I've heard of Playa-Hatin' between siblings, but for Mom to despise her offspring because Dom actually looks like an attractive young woman ***instead*** of the ungainly waif from high school she used to verbally abuse... **that** is a new one on me.

Dominique looked ***nothing*** like Dame Doom, the name many former classmates still use when talking about her; she went from thin, pale Goth with the ubiquitous midnight Black No.1 dye job to average dark-haired college beauty, thanks mostly to Lawrence Jules "L.J." Ellis. She also filled out, rather nicely I believe though I **am** partial to certain feminine body proportions. If I had to judge I'd place her at an easy 34-B cup on an athletic, trim body; if she maintains herself she'll be MILF once she turns twenty-five, and I don't mean she'll look old. There is wisdom etched in her features that goes far beyond her youthfulness and it drapes her entire body in a seductively warm yet fascinatingly dark aura. Though to be fair, there is a **reason** for the dark glow; at one time she was the pawn of a very evil entity.

"What brings you by, Alexander?" I watched as she poured two mugs of green tea, my favorite drink. She stared at them and I noticed her taupe hair blacken, taking on a slight blue tint like that seen on a raven in near-Spring sunlight.

"Lord Quick's departure from this city; he left the Back House open for you and the others."

"That's very gracious of him; did he return to New Orleans?" Her focus never wavers; I'm impressed by her control... and disturbed by how easily she uses her Gift. She is a full Psion, capable of manipulating energies normally called *magic;* she also possesses the Issues that brings, though it is incorrect to call her a true Wicca.

Witch is the preferred term, and it is one she only recently shies away from; she wears a simple sapphire ring and a diamond solitaire on a silver necklace, and while they pulsate with Power only another Psi-Witch or Empath could tell they were more than casual bling.

"He left; let's just leave it there. Have you heard from the others?"

"Marcus emailed me before he left." She fell silent, staring at the steaming mug of green tea. I heard the emptiness and knew why it hung in her throat: her former boyfriend L.J.

"I take it your break up wasn't easy then."

"It's not the break-up; something happened to him. I Feel it." She stared at her cup; I left her to her Thoughts, but not out of respect.

"Then why not contact him?" Dominique pulled her smart phone from the pouch of her college hooded sweatshirt, but didn't look at it. "Not that way, my dear..."

"No. I gave my Word not to; so did he." There it is: **WHY** I stayed out of her Thoughts...

"He is a Member of the Clan Cursed and Bound by his Word. You are not."

"That's what makes it so hard."

And completely understandable; I know full well what Love does to one of the Clan Cursed. Watching Dominique run her fingers through her hair reminded me of what *loving* one of the Clan Cursed did; there are kinder torments in this world and in no less than five of Hell's lowest levels.

"At any rate, I am here to give you the keys to the Back House... and warn you against entering Darkhaven Manor."

"Did something happen?" Her rich brown eyes flashed; silver flecks appeared and danced erratically within the iris as Power flowed through her entire body. I was truly... disturbed; her control was beyond masterful.

"Don't ask... and **don't** go prying into things, Miss Gordon. There is more than enough evil running rampant in your Home Town; given the current state of things, you and Lord Quick's Students will **need** someplace Safe." Of course I didn't expect her to listen; her Thoughts drifted to the Blackened Scroll and the dark knowledge it contains. If I'm right she'll open its pages and learn as much as possible. Smart **and** Beautiful; no wonder L.J. loves her. That combo will always be the downfall of any member of the Clan.

* * * *

She's hopeless. Dominique's mother assaulted her not two minutes after Alexander Charles Edwards left; the dark haired beauty fended off the barrage of questions without Anger filling her Thoughts. That was easily accomplished once Dominique realized her mother was also prying into Alexander's social status. *He would* ***never*** *think of getting cozy with any female in town.*

"Are you going out tonight at **ALL?!?!?**"

"Maybe later; right now I just wanna chill." Her mother's expression said she wasn't buying her daughter's words, but Dominique didn't care. She had plans for the night, and they required one thing above all else: knowledge. Ace's visitation brought several nagging questions from depths she didn't want to consider; while she wasn't surprised that Lord Silas Quick offered her, L.J. and Marcus the use of the Manor's guest house, she was curious as to why Ace warned her to stay away from the main building, Darkhaven Manor. Dominique punctuated her intent by flopping onto the sofa, snatching up the remote control and proceeding to flip channels.

"Well... I'm going to bed in a few; I've got work tomorrow."

"Sleep easy, Mom." Dominique smiled at her mother's gruff snort and continued flipping channels; nothing distracted her from her constant thinking. Eventually she turned the television off and quietly padded to her bedroom. Once inside she closed her eyes, back pressed against her bedroom door, and focused her churning thoughts on a clear, still lake. Her lips moved after several long heartbeats and the image changed; the lake began bubbling quietly. Slowly a small water eyeball rose from its depths; she gave the Construct commands and watched it float into a starless sky.

That'll take care of that; now to study up. Dominique slowly opened her eyes. Instead of Reality's bland sharpness her entire room glowed faint blue, indicating **something** attempted to pierce the formidable wards she'd placed over her room.

Powerful... and unskilled; Dominique frowned, scrutinizing every detail before her. Even the room's familiar scent underwent detailed analysis; scented candles and potpourri wafted through the central-heating filtered sterility. Perfume danced over Humanity's peculiar odor, and the ancient tomes in her possession burped musty old library; yet these were normal. What was not normal was the faint blue glow's presence; it remained steady, as if the powerful unseen attacker was constantly assaulting her wards with patient, even determination. And yet... with so much power being used, there was no real damage done; this worried the young woman. Satisfied that her wards were indeed holding she set about retrieving a few Artifacts from their innocuous hiding places; each one held immense Power and she used them skillfully. Dominique was a bit unnerved by the skill she displayed with her first Psionic incantation, and the sensation only deepened when it seemed ineffective; she performed several others, each one more intricate than the last. The aura eventually faded, but it did so with control betraying not only great skill but *intelligence*.

Dominique took a deep breath after reinforcing her wards; seconds later the mermaid picture over her bed made sounds: bubbles under water, indicating her mother was fast asleep. With her mother asleep there was little chance of being discovered and for a brief moment she toyed with simply walking out her front door. During her stay at college she avoided using her Gift; she did, however, study two of the three tomes she acquired from the library concealed beneath Darkhaven Manor. As she stared at the keys in her right hand she exhaled slowly, breathing the proper incantation; white mist/smoke faded into existence, swirling clockwise around her as she molded the Psionic energy. While much slower than Shadow Walking, her method provided one thing: warmth. Shadow Walking always left the psychology major feeling cold and slightly disoriented; she never mentioned this to L.J. for he seemed all **too** comfortable with the death-cold entering someone's Thoughts, a key element allowing Shadow Walking, brought. The smoke/mist rose silently; soon her small bedroom disappeared. Her eyes widened sharply as the air changed from lavender and furnace warm to shockingly cold outside wind. The smoke/mist vanished, blown away by howling winds; there before her startled eyes stood the guest house. She Felt Darkhaven Manor's ruthlessly cruel scrutiny behind her, though it wasn't where she remembered it being; she did not turn to confirm the Sensation however.

Welcome White Witch; it has been some time since you visited. The voice rumbled within her Mind, giving the appearance of its speaker being behind her and to the left. She smiled and bowed her head in that direction before Mind Speaking.

Thank you Grimfang; I hope the Pack is as strong as ever.

The Pack is Eternal, though I no longer serve as Alpha; that is for the Young and Strong... not the elderly and crafty.

Crafty I grant you, ELDERLY...

I am over two of your centuries old, White Witch; it was long overdue that another take my place.

Yet you still live...

I am Needed here; Hunt Well, White Witch.

Kill swiftly, Grimfang. Perhaps I may be allowed council with the new Alpha soon.

I will send word. The wind picked up slightly; Dominique bowed once more, acknowledging the ancient Psi-wolf's exodus from her Thoughts. Only then did she take a step forward. The wind receded momentarily, and she took a deep breath, tasting the air. There was always something magical in its flavor, and tonight was no different; yet there was more Darkness in it as well. She jingled the keys for a heartbeat, listening for some strange reply; a slow smile pulled at her lips as the porch light flickered. Instead of an electrical hum the flickering sounded like tiny wings fluttering: a sign that the pixies were still on the premises. She unlocked the door, which swung open with a soft groan, and entered the stylishly Spartan living room.

"M'lady witch... welcome back."

"Grort; I didn't expect to see you here." She watched as the oddly dressed house gnome clamored onto the loveseat's back. Tall for his race, he didn't wear the traditional pointed hat. He wore a black leather half-helm on his head and his long white hair exploded from beneath it, boiling over his back. A brilliant blue silk shirt covered his torso and over that he wore something very familiar: his tool vest; the soft black fabric held countless pockets, each filled with bizarre and ordinary tools. Yet it was his pants that drew her full attention; they were midnight black combat pants sized perfectly for his stubby legs... and a trademark of all Warrior Gnomes.

"I prefer your socks to your mothers; she reeks of cheap cologne." The round faced, bearded house gnome reached into one of his pants pockets and pulled out a single pink sock; he presented her long lost sock to her with genteel flourish, a broad smile twinkling within his warm blue eyes.

"Be careful!!" Dominique chuckled happily.

"Will the young Lords be stopping by? I've only seen to your room..."

"I'm not sure." She tried to keep Thoughts of L.J. from her tone as she tucked the sock inside her hooded sweatshirt's pouch.

"Very well; gives me time ta fill the kitchen properly then."

"Tell me you've not been reduced to mere Housekeeping, Grort the Stalwart."

"Hardly; I'm here because one of Lord Quick's students visits, nothing more. I'm in charge of the Manor now."

"Then he **has** left the city."

"Council business I suppose; the place is all boarded up. Only Spirits linger there, and I ain't too fond of the Dead, Lady Witch. Trom is head of this house; he's probably waiting to see what trinkets you bring." Grort bowed respectfully, leapt onto the floor and scurried to one of the book cases lining the wall, where he promptly vanished, leaving only the faint smell of her favorite laundry detergent.

CHILDREN OF TOMORROW

From the Blackened Scroll:

These are the known Psionic Gifts; though not in any specific order, the List covers the entire spectrum on abilities Past and Present.

* * * *

Remote Viewing

Largely considered the Harmless Gift, Remote Viewing grants the Psion the ability to witness events currently transpiring elsewhere. In some cases the *proper* phraseology is **Remote *Sensing***; four of the five physical senses are active. Only Touch is omitted from Remote Sensing; if Touch is present then the Gift is more accurately termed **Projection**.

As with all Gifts, Remote Viewing/Sensing and Projection are limited by the physical senses of the user. This leads to some interesting situations: those born blind cannot See, though their other senses, naturally heightened to compensate for the lack of physical sight, may well exist, giving them the ability to Hear words and sounds,

Taste and even Smell. Blind Projectionists can Feel things, yet they cannot discern the Color; nor can a blind Projectionist tell distance unless they are trained in echo location or some other distance measuring technique. Likewise, Projectionists born deaf cannot Hear; if they are skilled at reading lips they may understand some words. Also, if they are trained they may use their Touch-Sense to *feel* words and sounds, but it is inaccurate to say their Gift completely compensates for their physical deafness. Another curious limitation occurs with Projectionists; they can touch a doorknob but **cannot** turn it. However they can run their Touch over flesh and the Subject will feel the sensation **and** its movement along their flesh.

* * * *

Mind Reading

Many Mundanes consider this Gift the most horrifying; people have long believed their Minds to be the one Safe Place within the Human Form, and next to the Soul, the most impenetrable. Mind Reading is a limited Gift however; one possessing this Gift can **only** read from the Conscious Mind. The Subconscious Mind presents only scattered Images and Sounds and these are often disjointed or lack any tangible perspective. Mind Readers must also contend with the Cacophony; every Human Thinks, meaning discerning one Mind from another requires filtering out the constant mental chatter. This is further complicated by the fact that not everyone Thinks the same way. Infants think differently than teenagers; Adults think differently based upon their experiences. Someone born in Japan thinks differently than someone from China, India, Texas, England, etc. So a Mind Reader may indeed Read a Mind and be incapable of understanding the Thought.

* * * *

Energy Projection

Of all Psionic Gifts this is the most diverse; this is natural and should be obvious. Energy manifests in many different forms and those possessing this Gift are just as diverse. They are also differentiated due to **how** they control and manipulate the energies at their disposal. If there is one unifying detail, it lies within their limitation; all energy projectionists are limited by the Human Body. The Human Body can only withstand so much excess energy before it fails; the best analogy is a resistor in a circuit. Push too much current through it or apply too much voltage across it and the resistor burns; do likewise with Psionic-based energy and the human body will fail, the nature of which depends on the nature of the energy being projected as well as physical limitations such as frailty, illness and general health.

There is one matter which must be brought up; not all energy projectionists are limited to one form of energy. The most powerful energy projectionists have historically been called Witches, Wizards and Sorcerers, though only a few of those were true energy projectionists; the rest are merely victims of Human prejudice and ignorance.

Sound Projectionists are a curious example of Energy Projection; Sound can only exist where there are molecules available to transmit the energy. Thus it *should* follow that they are powerless in a vacuum; such is not the case, as they may use the sound generated by their own body (heartbeat... even gas) as a source from which to draw upon.

* * * *

Telekinetics

The power to move an object simply by Thought alone is the essence of telekinetics; what is seldom understood is the odd size limitation. It is fallacy to assume it takes more power to lift a large boulder than it does to pick up an ink pen. By and large, size limitation is a matter of perception; it's been shown that a blind T-K, to use the slang term, can move boulders as easily as the ink pen so long as no distinction is made between the two within his Mind.

Beyond a certain level, however, power takes a back seat to the Focus the telekinetic possesses; microscopic T-Ks are especially Focused individuals. They are also highly capable when it comes to visualizing things such as cells; this makes Micro T-Ks particularly dangerous... and valuable. A Micro T-K can constrict blood vessels or even cause blood cells to clump together, forming blood clots; while deadly, the range for this particular Gift is usually very limited: no more than thirty feet. Coupled with Remote Viewing, however, this limitation virtually vanishes.

There are two major limitations T-Ks express. One is called *Movement Allocation*; in order to use their Gift the T-K must move some part of their physical anatomy. The other is commonly referred to as *Stillness*; the T-K must remain perfectly still in order to properly Focus their Thoughts.

* * * *

Empaths

Ask any Psion what they consider the most powerful **and** dangerous Gift and they will probably say, "Empathy." As for why this is, the answer stems from its adaptability; before the Computer Age Empaths had only Minds and Souls beneath their influence. Now Humanity is virtually dependent upon its silicon processors; where once it could safely laugh about the Ghost in the Machine, today there are Empaths who view computers as Thinking, sentient creatures and interact with them as such.

Tech Head

A Tech Head is an Empath whose Gift is more attuned to computers and other machines. At the low end of this Gift the Psion can diagnose problems with a glance; the more powerful Tech Head possesses abilities coveted by many Government and Corporate entities. These include remote operation of vehicles, even those without computer guidance systems, such as bull dozers and automobiles, semi trucks, ships, boats and submarines.

Generics

Only Tech Heads call non-Tech Heads *Generics*; the term is only slightly derogatory, as there are Generics who view computers as less-than-sentient Life Forms such as dogs, cats and reptiles. Generic Empaths are, however, organic Life Form centric; here one discovers why the Term *Generic* isn't considered completely derogatory. Wizard,

Witch, Oracle, Shaman, Prophet, Sorcerer, Bokor... NECROMANCERS; these are some of the Terms used to describe a Generic Empath. Because of those Terms, it should be stated that nearly all man-made *'magical'* items are attributed to Generic Empaths; within the Psion community these items are properly termed **Artifacts**.

Generics is where one finds those known as the **Thrice Damned**; their Gift is attuned to the vast probability commonly called **THE FUTURE**. The Phrase Thrice Damned comes from this: they are aware of the **most likely** turn of events; because of the random nature of Life and Free Will there is no one Future. Over the course of Human History those with Future-Sight have been worshiped, hunted down and enslaved, or simply slaughtered, hence the Term **Thrice Damned**.

As for limitations... **all** Empaths suffer from some mental disorder. However, the greater the disorder, the more power the Empath has access to; put simply, the most dangerous and powerful Empaths are madmen/women. Many display symptoms of schizophrenia. An Empath's brain processes data differently than any other Psion or Mundane; this leads Empaths to suffer from a greater occurrence of brain tumors and aneurisms, even exceeding an energy projectionist whose power emanates from the brain.

Empaths are also highly susceptible to Ascension, though the success rate is difficult to qualify. The Soul may well remain coherent, but the Mind tends to shred into countless parts, and the physical form simply cannot maintain cellular integrity once the Ascension process begins; however, the combined Soul/Will of the Empath may be enough to bend the rules, though this does not decrease the possibility or intensity of any catastrophic results. One such result: Psionic irradiation; there also might be localized natural phenomenon such as earthquakes or intense storms. Yet the most devastating result of Ascension is one normally confined to Science Fiction literature; it's happened enough times that there is a Term for it: ***M'ash'I*** (pronounced: ***more-AHsh-shEE***). Briefly stated, this is what happens when several Realities/Universes are temporarily connected at points where the tremendous energy of Ascension tears through the barriers separating them; I know First Hand about the experience. It is not pleasant.

* * * *

It is possible for someone to possess multiple Gifts; the strain on Mind and Body are immense. Yet there are some Gifts which work very well together, and they create unique Psionic classifications.

* * * *

Surgeon

Surgeons have vast knowledge of the microscopic universe; like their mundane counterparts they carefully manipulate it to certain ends. **Unlike** modern surgeons they don't require physical tools such as scissors, retractors or even optics to magnify the area being worked on; they don't even need PET scans as they posses the ability to See the brain functioning in Real Time. The most skilled possess knowledge of anatomy far exceeding the most skilled Mundane Think Tank and are not limited to Seeing only the brain; for these Surgeons, the entire biological process within an organism is Seen as if watching a movie in Hi-Def Complete Surround (full 360 degree sight, sound and *touch*).

It doesn't take much to comprehend the darker aspect of such command and control: **Programming the Mind and/or Body**. While possible, only the Council possesses access to their skills currently.

* * * *

The Puppet Master

Of all Empaths the Puppet Master is the most feared. A common tale within Humanity is that of losing control over ones Mind and Body; Puppet Masters can remove the Conscious and Subconscious Mind from its normal role within the body and replace it with their own or carefully constructed Code. This Code is useful for controlling animals, adding even more Fear to an already terrifying reputation. Being attacked by a rabid dog or wild animal is one very real Human Fear; few want to contemplate the faithful Family pet suddenly turning into a savage killer. Perhaps the most common abuse of this Gift is for rape; forcing the Mind to experience every sensation of the physical nightmare *except* sight is something I've personally experienced. To me, there is no greater violation except Mind Raping. I've even dealt with a Puppet Master who turned a mild mannered person into a sociopath killer, leaving the Memory of the Puppet Master's crime available once the Mind returned to active control over the body; helping them put their shattered Mind back together was my first Assignment as a Council Member, and how I came to lead the Psions greatest, most terrifying asset: the **Soul Hounds**.

The most common Mundane examples of Puppet Masters are **Necromancers** and **Bokor**; both are given the power to animate the dead, yet one thing must be stated: they do ***NOT*** place Souls into corpses. Indeed, these Mundane characters have a common link in that they possess the ability to seal Souls away in non-living items; so, in a very real sense, Mundane lore reveals an intrinsic limitation all Puppet Masters possess: they can only **move** Souls from their living bodies and have no power to actually ***CREATE*** Souls.

* * * *

Soul Hounds

Soul Hounds (just *Hounds* in the vernacular) are Empaths capable of tracking someone by their Thoughts. The Term *Soul Hound* refers to those Hounds who can track the Soul itself. The Gift itself can be natural or the Empath can train himself/herself to become a Hound. With practice even a Mundane can cloud his Thoughts enough to throw off most tracking attempts. Hounds are skilled at discerning their Prey's baseline Thought pattern from any background Thought disturbances or any other confusing patterns (it is commonplace to have some Thought frequencies scrambled by electronic interference; this is due to the bio-*electrical* nature of brain impulses). Soul Hounds are less affected by this White Noise; they track the Soul, though how this is accomplished is still debated, even amongst Council members.

From Souls Hounds come the Council's most feared warriors: **Soul Killers**. With enough skill and power it is possible to leave Scars upon the Soul that will never fully heal; Soul Killers are rumored to be the only creatures in the Known **Universe** capable of actually *destroying* the Soul completely. In reality they shred the Soul beyond the point where it can regenerate or recombine; only God can destroy the Soul completely.

* * * *

The Ascended

What sets the Ascended apart from other Psions is difficult to define and impossible to confine within one specific concept or word. It is perhaps better to begin at **why** Psions become Ascended, and even here there is a great deal of controversy. This is due to the one consistent fact in all Ascended: ***the Soul refuses to die***.

This is what that statement means as far as my personal research can determine: the Psion's body is stressed beyond its breaking point and the Soul, drawing upon vast Psionic energy, refuses to allow the **physical** form to experience its natural demise. The controversy then becomes: *what happens to the physical form*; all Matter is Energy, yet the obvious answer of *it becomes a different energy form* is, and is not, correct. There is a perfect example of what happens to the physical form, but this example threatens the entire Christian Faith: **the resurrection of Jesus Christ**.

A close inspection of the Bible reveals that when Jesus reappeared his disciples did not immediately recognize him; therefore it is **logical** to conclude that Jesus' *physical appearance* was altered just enough to cause this discrepancy. I do not imply that Jesus was a Psion and Ascended, but it does reveal a common occurrence all Human Ascended share: ***the reconstituted Physical Form cannot mimic its previous state exactly***; my research leads me to believe that this is because of the laws dictating the physical properties of solid matter within this Universe. If one extends this to Jesus, one believes He was **limited** by these laws; I do not believe this to be the case. My research leads me to this unsettling conclusion: the discrepancy revealed in this tale is actually meant for future Humans who would experience Ascendance and, by default, the Oddity of Self.

The Oddity of Self is one commonality; another: the Ascended all possess multiple Psionic gifts. A third commonality is one many do not like discussing; eventually the Ascended grow away from the **need** for a physical body. The physical body requires constant maintenance and is subject to physical ailments and death; as a being comprised of pure energy, such things as food, water... even physical contact... become abstract concepts. Once this happens the ascended in a physical form tends to have characteristics similar to science fiction entities; for example: they don't breathe, eat or sleep unless the situation calls for such displays.

While it is true Empaths make up the vast majority of the Ascended, they are not the only Psions capable of surviving the transition; any Psion **can** become Ascended. Empaths tend to show greater propensity for *surviving* the massive power required, and even here, the reason is more speculation than actual fact. Speculation gives this: their Minds, already splintered by their Gift, are more capable of remaining *coherent* after the transition. Considering all Empaths suffer from some Mental Issue, use of the word coherent is, perhaps, pretentious. Therefore I choose to believe this: the combination of an Empath's Mind, Soul and Will maintains cohesion after the transition if **and *ONLY* if** that same combination has a very deep understanding of the nature of the Multiverse.

MORE THAN FOUR WALLS

Richard sat on the porch of his new house, the sketch pad resting in his lap as he studied the boarded up house across the street. He blinked several times, tilting his head so that his blonde bangs partially covered one eye; though it looked like the other empty houses in the area there was something ominously fascinating about the white building with a black awning shielding the bare front porch. The grass-and-weed front yard was neatly maintained, and the maple tree dominating one side of the yard looked wild and lovingly kept up; the house itself seemed to wait patiently, drawing slow, even breaths as it sat among the other eyeless buildings. Richard wiggled his pencil thoughtfully for several seconds before taking a deep breath and continuing his sketch; he ignored the silent approach from behind him, focusing on the lines and shades and shadows on the paper.

"Glad to see you drawing."

"There's someone in there," the thirteen year old said; he didn't look up at his mother, keeping his eyes focused on his drawing.

"Doubt it; come inside. I've got dinner ready."

Avril White pulled her sparkling eyes from the pencil drawing, smiling proudly at her only child. As she rose from her silent crouch she heard a cat mew; both turned towards a bush on her left. After several moments where the bush seemed to shudder/chuckle, a gray and black tabby poked its small head from its cover, the yellow eyes sparkling as it watched them warily.

"Hello to you!!!" Richard's voice was strong yet youthful and, Avril noticed, lacking its recent somber undertone. "Is this your home?" The mew/guttural growl/purr rumbled softly.

"If you take it as yours it stays outside, son."

"I don't think he'd stay inside for very long."

"He?"

"Yep. This is my mom; Mom... this is Grey Shadow."

"Hello Gray Shadow!!"

"No, Mom... GREY - G, R, **E**, Y."

"I'm sorry!!" It pleased her to see him actually show interest in the stray cat and she began to hope their recent troubles were beginning to fade.

"Can we find him something to eat... and can he stay inside tonight? I think he's the runt of the litter."

"Of course." As her son crept over towards his new friend Avril turned her eyes towards the house across the street; she thought she saw something move on the porch.

"That's the Ghost of his father: Dada Boo Lazy Bones," her son said smoothly. "He roams around waitin' for his Human Friend... someone called Lord Quick." She smiled; warmed by her son's imagination. She overlooked the matter-of-fact Tone that served as their foundation; a child that *didn't* reach for some fantasy after such a disturbing, trying situation as they'd endured was cause for serious concern. This... was the beginning of healing.

* * * *

* * * *

L.J. let his eyes wander slowly around his bedroom; his Thoughts drifted to his recent past as a Driver for Lord Silas Quick. He missed the constant excitement of sliding through the Night with some self-important VIP huddled in the back seat doing their level best to be ignored, but not enough to return to the Thoughtscape and visit his mentor and boss immediately. His last assignment before the previous Summer nearly cost him his life and sanity; his chest tightened as the Memory exploded like a flash-bang.

"Son? Everything OK?"

"Yeah... just... thinking." L.J. chastised himself for not closing his bedroom door even though he Sensed his father's approach long before the elder Ellis spoke.

"At least you're not as jumpy as before, I was afraid I'd spook ya." L.J. chuckled; there was no way his father could surprise him. Between his training by Lord Silas Quick and his experiences tracking down Mutates in the Thoughtscape, being caught off guard was something the young man expected only Death itself could possibly do. Besides... there was still that creaky piece of floor between his room and his father's; even with the blue-and-green throw rug covering it, the slender young man Felt it give beneath his father's bulk.

"Guess I grew up." A tight smile winched L.J.'s lips; he inhaled briefly before snorting a sad sigh. The true weight of his words seemed like a sudden physical burden, and L.J. felt old; not older... just **OLD**.

"That happens if ya keep livin'; that your new company car?"

"Huh... wanna take it for a spin?"

"Nope; figured **you'd** wanna take a drive... clear ya head a bit."

L.J. turned towards his father smoothly; they were never really close and L.J. couldn't **remember** the last time he saw this much concern in those slightly weathered features. While it looked natural there was something in the way his father's eyes twitched; there was nervous tension tugging at his gaze... and there was none of the old Hustler hardness within his deep blue eyes. L.J. lowered his head and exhaled, closing his eyes in an exaggerated blink; while it appeared the young man was exasperated, his action concealed his true intention: Searching for any Psionic influence on his father.

"Yeah... probably gonna swing by Dom's house... see if she's in. Girl troubles are a pain."

"Tell me about it," his father chuckled.

*Hematite, and it reeks of Michaelson and Section 8; what the fuck are **they** doin' in my dad's house.* With a Thought L.J. entered his father's mind; when he encountered the Thought Wall he drew up sharply. ***DEFINITELY** gonna have a nice long chat with that old fucker; putting up a Wall in my dad's Thoughts isn't nice.*

"Lemme change first... and thanks dad... for everything." His father smiled... *sadly...* then sauntered down the hallway, heading for the master bedroom.

* * * *

From the Blackened Scroll:

On Artifacts

So... what exactly is an Artifact? While there are many famous examples, it is the lesser known Artifacts which cause the greatest difficulty. These Artifacts are more commonly called **Talismans, Charms** and **Cantrips**.

In the simplest form, an Artifact is *anything* which contains Thought energy; this includes a child's favorite toy, embedded with fond, happy memories. It includes favorite clothing articles, tools and even random items considered Lucky or special, such as Lord Silas Quick's ever-present black Bic Lighter or the Zippo lighter carried by ones grandfather during the war. These items are vessels imbued with Thought energy, and the Source of those Thoughts need not originate from a Psion; nor are Artifacts limited to Human Thought energy. A favorite pet's walking collar is just as powerful as the rock a child picked up during its favorite vacation; the main requirement is that the **THOUGHTS** are Focused and intense.

So it should come as no surprise that many Mundane artifacts are created accidentally; a famous example of this is the fabled Dead Man's Hand: Aces and Eights. Nor should the concept of Luck be easily dismissed in creating Artifacts, *especially* those items considered Unlucky or Cursed. Negative Thought energy is just as potent in creating Artifacts as positive energy; it is also accessed with greater ease. This is due to the nature of the known Universe as well as negative Thought energy's tendency to escape its confines.

Purposefully creating an Artifact takes much more than Thinking; the Will must mold and shape the Thoughts into cohesive patterns. One good example is the creation of the Living Doll; the legends vary, but one detail is almost universal: a Child. With this one detail one sees not only Imagination, but Belief; it must also be stated that *disbelief* is nothing more than **negative** Belief, which may account for the Adults in such legends inability to perceive Living Dolls as well as such Artifact's seeming hatred for Adults.

* * * *

The one thing about Section 8 L.J. remembers most: they are typical Government Agents when all's said-and-done. They tend to treat the general Public with little respect and expect their well thought-out plans to instill terror and awe, insuring compliance and silence within everyone beneath their thrall; that's difficult to do when he's danced with demons and possesses mental abilities far beyond their meager training. The hematite was hidden in the attic and possessed Shield Thoughts; so long as it remained in the house his father's mind was off-limits to his skill, or so Michaelson and Section 8 hoped. While he got dressed for the cold night he let his Thoughts Flow outside, testing the Artifact's power. He wasn't surprised or impressed; the round hematite chunk was highly polished... by someone with no idea *why* they needed to be so precise.

Never lose Focus when creating an Artifact he recalled from training with Lord Quick; he could easily destroy it, but decided to leave it in place. There was time enough to pry into its secrets; right now he was more concerned about the forceful Thoughts slamming into his home from outside. Two police officers sat in a patrol car, their Thoughts jumping from his new ride to the house. Before college he had only a passing dislike for cops; after one cowboy decided he needed to shake the

Fear of God into him because he was dating a black female and another sleazeball ended up running a kiddie-porn ring he smashed, he began to take Lord Quick's attitude: if they want War... given them Armageddon. As he slid his white hooded sweatshirt over his head he formed a series of *kuji-in*, his fingers moving with rapid ease as his Mind swirled with Thought energy. As the hood settled over his head he jerked his arms down, completing the necessary sequence. Outside the patrol car went utterly dark. He'd drained the battery and the EM pulse-fried their radios; he enjoyed their confusion and toyed with Sending Panic into their minds.

Enough damage for one night, Penance.

Lord Quick!!

I'm impressed with your restraint; I was about to sic a gremlin on them. How ya been, chummer?

Not bad; do you know why Section 8...

The cops have it in their head that I'm head of a new gang in town.

So... Section 8...

Decided to see if you knew anything about the Horde. I laughed out loud, tucking my wallet into my pants.

If anything, they should blame Marcus and I, not you; I didn't think the Horde had any members around

here... other than the ones we've helped Emerge. And Horace's family moved didn't they?

Yes. The Assassins refer to the African American males seen wearing black rosaries; they've Violated two young males who were out and about and both knew more about their Civil Rights than the Assassins thought proper. Worse, at least in their myopic minds, was the answer both gave when asked what Set they claimed.

"I Follow a Code; no wonder that cop back at the store couldn't get her mind off Silas." L.J. muttered softly. When the Bloods took over the East Coast gang scene Necropolis found itself **packed** with kids wearing red and claiming Blood; true to Southern Tradition they ignored it, figuring it was nothing more than the latest Rap Fad. That was stupid, especially when you know the city is notorious as a stop-over point along the Cocaine Corridor running from New York to Miami and west to Atlanta. Then again, so long as the *violence* and ***killing*** stayed outside of City Limits or was sanctioned by the rich white Purveyors, the *real* Power Players don't give a flyin' fuck. And, of course, they got their cut of the profits; Money runs every City and Necropolis is no different.

Do I need to take precautions then?

You don't but Dominique might if you two are still an item; watch over your Friends, Penance.

"Son?"

"Yeah, Dad?" *Will do Lord Quick, and could you do something about that Shield Artifact? I think it's polluting my father's Mind.*

It is, and I've already moved it; the Free Talent responsible for it apologizes.

Lord Quick's Thought Speech Felt hideously cold and utterly remorseless; whoever the Free Talent was, they were gasping for breath as Meanstreak choked Life from their body. *Sucks to be that fucker.*

"Here. I... I was gonna wait until Christmas to give you this."

"Uncle Mike's K-Bar? Dad... I can't take this..."

"Please." **NOW** L.J. was scared; he looked at the knife his father held reverently. He Hears it whisper softly, but wasn't too surprised; it'd been in Vietnam and wars have a way of creating Artifacts. "I don't like the idea of you runnin' the streets without something ta protect ya." He *tried* to sound flippant but there was too much Fear in his tone and the words came out slightly choked.

"Thank you." L.J. meant his Words; he felt tears swelling in his eyes and quickly choked down his emotions, though he Felt their Power envelope them when they hugged. "I haven't gotten you anything..."

"You're in college and doin' well; keep livin' and doin' ya best. That's present enough, son." He nodded.

One more thing, Lord Quick; MAKE THAT FUCKER SUFFER!!! My father isn't perfect by a long shot, but I never **once** imagined he actually cared this much about me. He chased skirts and drank beer and moonshine like a professional Drunk; while L.J. was pleased he'd gotten better he wasn't exactly thrilled about *why* he chose to get better. God's intervention or he just decided to do better... he'll accept; some idiot in a suit and tie pouring raw Fear and who knows what else **directly** into his mind: No.

If there's anything left I'll keep it in storage for you. Now... behave yourself Penance; and remember what I asked.

Watch over my Friends... and Family; he moved down the stairs silently, Uncle Mike's K-Bar sleeping in the worn leather sheath. He shifted it into his right hand and blinked slowly, Summoning his duster and black rosary from the Manor. He hit the bottom step and stopped, the heavy armored duster oddly comforting as it fell over his body; he looked down at his chest and smiled faintly. The image of the Virgin Mary still bore the scar from the demon's hellish talons. He stepped off the stairs and swooshed into the living room; as he reached for his black baseball cap he caught a glimpse of himself in the flat-screen. Somehow his hood, which he'd removed from his head upon hearing his father's voice, was back on... **and the Face of Penance** glowed ghostly white before fading away, leaving his slightly puzzled face staring back at him.

* * * *

* * * *

Dominique smiled as the shower eased her tension. The room she occupied has a full bathroom and she often joked that her friends put her there because they didn't like waiting for bathroom time. The athletic young woman rinsed her toned body, turning off the water as she reached for the shower curtain; soft, melodious bells tinkled, and Dominique shifted her Senses.

"Thank you; please show him inside." The small pixie danced in the air, blushing as it turned its tiny head away while she dried off. After quickly donning a pair of pink jogging pants and a matching over-sized long sleeved tee-shirt she slipped into a pair of white bunny slippers and headed downstairs. She stopped on the staircase, looking down as several house gnomes crowded around Silas Quick, clad in a black cloak and looking rather handsome, though a bit haggard with his scruffy near-beard. She noticed a few silver/gray hairs jutting wildly from both sides of his neck; they added a few years to his appearance, but not enough to suggest his true age.

"Well met Lord Quick!"

"Salutations Dame Dominique; how was your trip home?"

"Exhausting. I'd heard you were not in town."

"Officially I am not, though I will always have time for my former students." Polite as always, his tight-lipped smile pleased her... even as it reminded her of L.J., who adopted many of Lord Quick's mannerisms while they dated.

"Is this a social call?"

"In a manner of speaking; I've come to alert you to matters which may find their way to your doorstep." She watched as his brow furrowed slightly; moments later a large dark shadow silently appeared and Marcus' form faded into existence, hovering several inches above the floor and clad in a college sweatshirt and slightly baggy black denim jeans.

"Dominique... and Lord Quick!! Shadows Guard you, Lord of Darkhaven Manor."

"Shadows Guard, Marcus!!"

"**Marcus!!!!** Is something wrong?"

"Actually... I'm not sure; my girlfriend's mother Smells like that seduction potion you whipped up back in the day. Carrie's grandmother is a Psi-witch named Hazel..."

"You **do** have problems old friend; Witch Hazel and I have tangled before."

*"Sounds like **you've** had a busy school year. Maybe that explains how she recognized me as a Hound."*

"Indeed?" quipped Silas. "Then you should definitely be on your guard, only the Council is aware of who serves as a Hound."

"Witch Hazel's a nosy slut."

"DOM!!!!"

"It's true; her Seduction potions are very powerful and the old hag **keeps** a stable of young studs to satisfy her."

"Guess I can expect Carrie's father to no-show for sure; if you have anything that'll prevent her potion from kicking in I'd be grateful."

"Give me two hours... unless you have an idea, Lord Quick."

"Unfortunately I cannot intervene in this matter. I **can** connect you with a Tech Head; your surroundings are monitored by a dedicated closed-circuit security system. Be careful where you Shadow Walk; the visual range of most cameras is much broader than Human Eyesight. You'll leave Ghost Trails."

"Thanks for the reminder Lord Quick. I'll see you in a few, Dominique."

"Before you leave..." Dominique reached towards the turning image of her friend and Adopted Brother; Marcus paused, and she bit her bottom lip as Darkness wavered over his strong features.

"No word from him yet; Shadows Guard you both." Dominique sighed.

"Don't sound so defeated; L.J. has issues of his own, though that isn't quite accurate. Seems the local law enforcement believes I'm the leader of a new gang in town and are looking for him **and** Marcus; if they aren't watching you they'll start soon."

"Thanks for the warning." Dominique turned and took a seat on the large sofa; Silas walked over to the front window silently.

"Tell me: why do you want to see L.J.? I know you care deeply for him, but your actions suggest you Sense something is wrong."

"I don't know. It's nothing I can put my finger on, and I **won't** use my power to pry." She lowered her voice before continuing. "Not that I could..."

"Never underestimate the Power of Love, Dame Dominique. Call him; be brave. Eventually he'll check up on you, if only to make sure no one is spying on you."

"That will make it Business; he gets..."

"Cold and ruthless; that is the Way of the Clan Cursed my dear. Remind him of his Humanity... every chance you get." The enigmatic black man strode towards, then through the window; hot on his heels the House Gnomes followed, each one dropping a small item they'd acquired from their brief stay. The small pile almost made her smile; House Gnomes were notorious for *acquiring* **one** of every paired item within a household.

* * * *

* * * *

Carrie's home reminded Marcus of Darkhaven Manor in many ways. Not only was it tucked well away from any major or minor road but the journey to her large mini-mansion was vaguely reminiscent of walking along one of the many deer trails in Necropolis. Imposing trees, some with defiant leaves clinging to bare branches, littered the landscape; the dark night only added to their gruesome appearance and ominous beauty as scant star light dripped through faint, feathery purple clouds, dying leaves and crooked branches. The six-foot tall African American gazed over the large back yard, flicking his eyes to the wild, natural tree tops clawing at the mysteriously seductive night sky. He left his introspection the instant his Senses, honed by constant study as a Soul Hound, detected the silent movements and too-loud Thoughts of an intruder behind him. Marcus lowered his gaze to his right hand side and snorts a soft chuckle, his breath just beginning to gray into mist as the temperature dropped another degree. He waited until the sliding door behind him ceased moving before speaking, his deep voice soft and, he hoped, soothing.

"Beautiful... just like you, Carrie."

"Thank you." Musical and playful as always, Marcus couldn't help but notice the surprise in her gentle tone. "Mom's got dinner ready; come inside."

Playful seductress as always; wonder when she's gonna break out the weed. Marcus suspected something was up when he caught her talking to one of the cooks from another restaurant; naturally paranoid he'd entered the Thoughtscape in order to Hear their conversation and was slightly surprised that his girlfriend was buying marijuana. He smoked, but more to fit in with the other cooks; he wasn't sure what her mother, Daphne, would think of the drug and wasn't sure **where** his girlfriend would suggest they blaze. The brief tour of her large, skillfully decorated home suggested they'd be lounging in the indoor Jacuzzi, but there was one very big concern ripping through his mind: he'd spotted several hidden security cameras within her home. **There are no cameras within the Manor, but you are *ALWAYS* being watched**; Marcus didn't like the aggravatingly creepy Feel within Darkhaven Manor and Carrie's home had a similar feeling when he entered, so he studied his unfamiliar surroundings carefully. After Lord Quick's warning he opted for Hound Paranoia, scrutinizing and memorizing every minute detail.

"Who lives over there?" Marcus indicated the thin smoke column winding its way skyward.

"Auntie Marge and Uncle Matt; they live on the other side of the woods. They might be over tomorrow if the storm doesn't dump too much snow. I hope they do; I really miss Little Joey. I think you'll like him; he's as paranoid as you are, and he **loves** wandering through the woods."

"How old is he?"

"Fifteen goin' on fifty!!" He blended his soft laughter with her joyous utterance, swept her up in his left arm and headed inside. As he did so his eyes caught sight of the slight color change betraying the approaching snow storm; right before the sliding door closed he paused. Though only for a brief moment, it was more time than necessary for a Soul Hound; something was outside and it was *THINKING* about him. Deep within his Mind something breathed deeply, the Sensation cold and heartless; Marcus pulled the blinds over the sliding glass doors and backed out of the bedroom, turning with a predator's liquid grace only when he was at the door's threshold.

* * * *

Calvin Dobson isn't the best Tech Head I've come across, just the most scrupulous. It marks him as an outsider among his Louisiana high school classmates and he gets teased about it relentlessly. Depression crushed him until he saw his suffering affect his mother; she was still shaken by her husband's brutal assault and watching her only child fall deeper into depression, a hereditary condition, was more than she could bear. His emergence happened as he struggled to save her from her suicide attempt; he succeeded, becoming a powerful Empath in the process. Child of Technology he snatched up his smart phone and swore when he got no reception; shaking the device violently he Willed it to connect to the tower, and was surprised by what happened.

I was in the area when his Emergence happened; I was Hunting a Tech Head responsible for stealing several life savings, and the scumball showed himself as the young man stared at the electron ether before him. After securing my Prey I offered to help Calvin, and was surprised that he knew something about me; to be precise, he knew about the Horde. To him they were a loose knit group of young males who found something kindred within a particular writing I posted one year after surviving Hurricane Katrina's vengeful fury: **The Litany of the Lost**. He was thrilled by his new-found Gift and asked me to train him; while I am limited in Tech Head skills I did instruct him on how to control the Power flowing through his young Mind, as well as describe some of the Issues he encountered... such as his inability to Mind

Speak without his Bluetooth, and how to overcome some of those limitations.

Greetings Young Pup!!

Lord Quick!! What's up?

*Not much *chuckle*; how are you and your mother doing?* His restraint was impressive; most people look around when they hear a Voice inside their heads. Calvin muttered softly and adjusted his position on the couch as if he was struggling to remain awake... which **happened** to be the truth of the matter.

Mom's doing much better, thank you; she's still worried Dad will find her.

He won't be bringing pain to you or her for a very long time; I have a job for you... Over-Watch for one of my Pack... a Hound.

Sounds simple enough...

Nothing is ever simple, especially where I'm concerned. My former student will be visiting you within the hour to give you the details; he'll be Sending you an image of himself.

Thanks for the warning; do all Hounds Shadow Walk? Fear filled his Voice; he views Shadow Walking as pure Magic, and isn't quite sure it isn't Black Magic.

Not all; his name is Marcus. Please greet him properly and extend whatever assistance you can.

Done Lord Quick; I've been practicing hard.

If things go well you will consider this easy Work; though I warn you: My Pack seldom Hunts in safe places. And ***easy*** *is, whenever I say something is easy, a very relative term.*

* * * *

Calvin was impressed by Marcus' Sending; it looked like those three-dimensional images used in the Star Wars movies, only without the horizontal lines marking it as obvious technology. His Sending wore a shimmering black silk shirt and matching pants; his shoes were shiny black and spotless, but there was something odd: he never turned his back and kept his hands behind him. Calvin asked him to teach him how to do it, Send his Image to someone that way; he'd tried Shadow Walking, but there's no **way** he'd do it unless there's a ***SERIOUS*** emergency. To the young dark haired youth the Thoughtscape is beyond cold; if Death has a temperature setting it **has** to be the same as the Thoughtscape: Bone-chilling, Soul-draining **COLD** that never seems to stop. He didn't know if he was a fast learner or Marcus was an ***AWESOME*** teacher, but in no time he had his rough Avatar constructed and was on his way.

He entered the house via the power lines; maybe it was him, but he expected more fluctuations in the sixty cycles, if only because they were stuck on a mountain somewhere west of the Boonies and he was stuck in Louisiana. The house security system had a **killer** firewall and a top notch virus program. Pity it was a local company running their programs on an off-the-shelf computer protected by a Prime Password; ***God*** should **never** be used as a password. Even newbies know to start with Prime Passwords first; while he wasn't some super-geek Hacker, he had skills only a few people can dream of... outside of science fiction writers that is. What he found really odd was the remote access terminal in the basement; it sent data to a relay computer on the other side of the mountain and from there the signal went through the standard networks until it reached an office building in a town some distance from the house. And **that** computer has a remote access program tasked to send the data to two mobile devices; the passwords on that computer were better, but still whole words. Someone went through a lot of trouble to not only get the data, but very *little* effort was spent on hiding the trail.

What have we here? Guess daddy wants to keep his eye on things at home; if the snow storm knocks power out he'll be in the dark. Marcus: you hear me?

Loud and clear; any trouble from Spirits?

None so far; can they ***really*** *affect an electronic signal?*

You don't watch those paranormal shows on TV, do you; the ones where some group of so-called professionals go lookin' for ghosts?

I prefer to keep my horror confined to cheesy flicks. Marcus huffs out a rough chuckle before Speaking.

You should; Ghosts and other spirit manifestation can be seen by and have limited interaction with some electronic devices.

Swell; lemme run down the system before I get a surprise. Every room has at least two cameras, including the bathrooms and the Jacuzzi. That place even has two placed under water, which made me take a second look at the entire house. I think someone has serious Sex-on-the-Brains; their placement gives the viewer access to some porn-quality angles. Some of the cameras have a zoom-function as well.

You're too young to know about PORN... but that fits the intelligence I have; how many secret rooms are there?

Two; both are in the basement. There's also a secret area in the main bedroom located in a closet. Found that by comparing the file online with the contractor who designed the place with the dimensions I measured out. Can I ask... what's your Prey?

I AM the Prey this time; you've done great work for a rookie.

Thanks... I think; I'm still getting used to Command Chair operations, not to mention Mind Speaking. At least I'm almost over needing a Bluetooth in my ear to do it.

Yeah; welcome to the Wide World of the Strange and Twisted, rookie. Question: did Lord Quick teach you how to store data while circumventing hardware limitations?

Sure; still don't know why.

Check your back pack's inside pocket; there's a jump drive there. And check for a power generator connected specifically to the cameras and the computer running it... Marcus' Thought-Voice changed with each bit of information; the low growl he used for breathing **really** spooked Calvin, and set him up for what happened next.

One moment while I see... ***SHIT!!!***

It hung in the air, staring at the bank of batteries; Hollywood hadn't prepared him for what a ghost really looks like. Thankfully Marcus was there... or at least part of him was... he **thought**; a black mass appeared before him as the ghost turned to face him.

What is it?

A Wandering Soul; he won't harm you. He's just drawing Warmth from the batteries; put your Mind back

into the power lines rookie. You're Projecting, and that energy signature is** far **more appealing to the Dead.

Roger THAT; what do I call you when you're on assignment.

Call me Chains. Now... check your back pack; plug the jump drive into your laptop and set up a program to dump the video feed from the cameras into it.

*That's a **LOT** of data; how must storage does the drive have?*

Ten thousand terabytes.

HOLY!!! Standard magnetic hard drives were just beginning to touch the one terabyte threshold... and Calvin had a small, innocuous jump drive that looked like it came from Wal-Mart... perfectly capable of storing ten thousand times as much data!!! But... he didn't put it there!!! Calvin was definitely in the Realm of Strangeness now.

MOVEMENT IN THE NIGHT

Everything looks different at night. Take the new *company* car parked in front of my home; the Audi **IS** different from the Honda Lord Quick had modified into the Wraith series... and the physical differences are *not* what I'm talking about. A Wraith was still a Honda, and you couldn't really shake the sense that the owner was on a budget and paranoid (no chrome and nearly black tinted windows); the Audi screams Business Executive or Money-in-the-Family. Drape both in Necropolis Night and suddenly they take on a powerful, ominous aura; most of that comes from the paint which is specially formulated to absorb certain electromagnetic frequencies. But it doesn't account for the low, predatory crouch they assume come nightfall; that stems from the other modifications, things the automotive industry **and** the Federal Government would be terrified of if they knew about. There was an orange street light nearby and if you looked from it to *either* vehicle it seemed weaker than if there was a different vehicle there... like light itself was **afraid** to shine too brightly in its presence. If there was any tell tale difference between **my** A6 and the stock model it had to be the headlights; they *looked* the same, but my ride did away with the annoying LED lights lining the headlight's belly. Oh... and the headlights themselves: they looked more like dragon's eyes than the stock car's random-angry-beast.

As I made my way to my new ride I spotted the police cruiser; even though it wasn't directly beneath a street light it glowed, giving away its position easily... something I doubted the Assassins inside its protective shell understood. Movement caught my eye, and I stared at the human-shaped dark figure; on any other night I'd chalk it up as one of the many Hustlers making their way through the streets. I squinted, shifting my sight into the Thoughtscape; there the figure looked completely different. Spirits have a distinctive appearance within the Thoughtscape's vast beyond-blackness; the middle-aged man paused, turning his head (and **only** his head). I pulled my Sight from the Thoughtscape after bowing slightly and respectfully; still looking in the same direction I saw no figure, only the rose bush and maple tree where he should have been... and where the Assassins, now free of their vehicle's confines, headed with their typical *time-to-get-a-Nigga-Notch* cocksure strut. One bellowed, "Hey you!" Moments later he was screaming at the Spirit to stop while breaking into a full run, his partner pausing just long enough to glance at the disabled cruiser before joining the pursuit.

I didn't wait until they were out of sight before opening the driver side door; if anyone saw me they'd assume I'd left the door unlocked because of how I just reached for the door handle. If they were particularly observant they'd also notice that the interior lights didn't come on; only a close inspection during the day reveals the blatant betrayal of just how different the car is: **NO** door handles... on a four-door sedan!! I used to think the missing door handles were dangerous; knowing what I know about the Wraith series cars I understand why they aren't there: security. You have to have a Psionic key, and **that** is only kept within the Mind and Soul. Once inside my new ride, Necropolis disappeared, replaced by sensors and screens packed with every imaginable data stream; I smiled grimly: this is how Meanstreak sees the Human Reality. Everything measured and known... all for the purpose of staying twenty-two steps ahead of everyone and everything; I know he isn't alive, and at times like this I'm glad he's on my side. The data stream is packed with data a Killer needs: escape routes... who resides in what building... who is actually *there*, and a constant transcript of police and fire crew frequencies. So when I spotted the small screen dedicated to Section 8, I took time to focus my scattered Thoughts on it; less than an instant later the windshield became a head's up display and I went from fighting depressing Thoughts to fending off rapidly growing paranoia.

Which makes driving around the city a stupid remedy; once Night claims the city the cops fan out in search of anyone they can safely Violate. So I naturally took the *cure-poison-with-poison* approach and stuck to the narrow side streets... places the Street Hunters, or Street Crimes Units, stalk. If you live on such a street and even so much as stick your head out of **YOUR** front door while they're nearby you'll get Violated; according to local wisdom and tradition, only people who are up to no damn good ***ever*** set foot outside once the sun goes down. I kept my eyes peeled for anything; after four streets I included the Thoughtscape immediately around the general area, and nearly drowned in the unfocused Paranoia. Once I got clear of that Fear funk I cranked the music and put as much distance between myself and the Psionic overload as possible.

Eventually I turned off the radio, frustrated by the bland tunes and constant advertisements that poured into the car's interior. The city hadn't change, and I chided myself for expecting *anything* to change in Necropolis; the City Managers and Old Money refused to **allow** Change to infiltrate their domain and actively hounded anyone attempting to bring it within spitting distance of their pristine Lie. Night-time Downtown was still devoid of any real life; unless a stumbling drunk or crack head peeled themselves from the dark shadows, nothing alive moved... not even the few trees kissed by stiff pre-Winter winds. The wires holding signal lights tried shrugging off the laws of physics; dead leaves chased phantoms in circles, dipping into darkened corners only to emerge with more dead foliage and the occasional plastic bag. There was a time when those signal lights would blink one color at night; someone with money complained and they now scream one solid color after 22:00. Cruising by the hospital I saw a few more living beings: mostly nurses, patients and those few who sought treatment in the Emergency Room. I didn't peer inside; hospitals and nursing homes are places where Death holds court and his Presence chokes the air from my lungs.

I made my way to the community college, eyes constantly scanning the road and sidewalks; to my right and about a quarter-mile distant is my old high school. I smile slightly as Memories flit across my mind. I'm distracted by headlights appearing across the intersection. A patrol vehicle with one Assassin whose Thoughts slaver for Action was stopped; I expected them to follow as I made my turn. For a while they did, but the car turned left after less than a mile, heading towards the Old Projects; the Thoughts were rude and racist, so I knew some African American was about to have their Civil Rights violated: business as usual in Necropolis... and most large cities if my Travels are any indication. I turned, putting the community college campus on my left side; ahead on my right I spotted two bodies dressed for the Streets first, the cold second. I know a blunt/beer run when I see it: the closest Head only looked at my car long enough to identify it as Police or Friendly while the other dropped his head, pulling bare hands from his pockets to adjust his hood on his dome. The neighborhood ahead and to the right is fairly quiet; if I wanted more Shadow Action I would turn left, heading towards the campus' rear buildings and the housing complex on the other side of the street.

I wasn't exactly driving aimlessly; this wasn't Recon either, though I've driven this particular route several times for that specific purpose. I turned right and made my way towards the old textile mill; there's a large park nearby. My father talked about what it was like in the Old Days, saying it was where Blacks went for their Weekend Cruising; now it's a place to get jumped by a crack head or raped. I didn't spend a great deal of time dipping through the streets here; keep going straight and I'd find myself in North Carolina, so I turned around and headed towards the university and the Enclave. If I wanted to attract a patrol car and possibly get Violated, the Enclave is second only to the remaining Projects. The Enclave is where the city's Old Money call home and I got my wish two minutes after turning into one tree covered street. The only thing preventing complete fulfillment was the donk boomin' hardcore rap as it rode through the area; I sighed as the patrol car sped by me. The passenger cop never looked my way, Focused and agitated as they prepared to rumble with another drug runner/dealer; I Searched the Thoughts within the donk and chuckled: they were a decoy. Riding Clean, they'd get a ticket for the noise and get stuck while the cops dragged out the drug dogs; fortunately for them the cops didn't have a plant-stash on them. Just another night in the pristine gem called Necropolis; disgusted, I plotted my trip towards Riverside Drive and the mega gas-and-go at its far end.

Riverside Drive is the Main Drag in Necropolis, running East to West along the city's main divide, the river. I never thought about how the area looked before the neon and squat buildings corrupted the land; now all I see is Humanity's viral input as I made down the road on the opposite side of the river towards the MLK bridge. As I approached Down Town I saw headlights here and there, moving at various speeds as the cars and other vehicles sliced through the Night; I passed five cars total by the time I reached the other side of MLK and connected with Riverside drive, each one containing two people with males behind the wheel. I recognized only one car-and-driver, shaking my head as the Mustang growled past; the driver's family made its money running moonshine and he's well known for making Milk Runs from the county into the city proper. I saw a cherry passed from passenger to driver in another and wondered if the cops would stop that vehicle; two **blacks** performing the same task: in a heartbeat. Two clean cut white kids in the BMW from the car lot owned by the driver's well-connected daddy would **only** be stopped if the vehicle swerved, was speeding or otherwise presented an obvious danger. I was driving **ISM - Internal Stealth Mode**; that means anyone trying to look into the vehicle, even through the windshield, would only see darkness. The new system in the car takes it one step further; they'd see a *shape* but couldn't positively place it as Male or Female and race is **utterly** out of the question. Of course, **THAT** would normally get the car stopped; once they scanned my license plate, however, they'd quickly find someplace else to be... ***normally***. I remembered the cops parked outside my home and adjusted the stealth settings.

I did very little button pushing; I'd driven the Wraith series cars long enough to grasp the controls naturally. So I was surprised when I noticed *Forms* on the large tablet-like monitor; I flipped through the selections, chuckling at a few odd selections. I *seriously* doubt anyone would believe a white-haired grandmother barely capable of looking over the steering wheel would drive a vehicle I **know** the cops have placed as belonging to Silas and his publishing company, Thoughts Consolidated. I opted for Clear View Plus as I knew I'd attract *some* attention from the police and really didn't want the hassle, especially on Riverside Drive where they tended to be complete dicks to any young person in a shiny black vehicle with shiny chrome and colored headlights (a crisp, unnatural blue-white light that mimicked halogen or LED lights perfectly for anyone without Psionic augmented vision). I passed by two patrol cars parked in a parking lot near my destination and sure enough they had someone pulled over; college kids home for the Holidays make easy targets for harassment. As I pulled into the gas-and-go I spotted a few familiar faces and two police officers; I heard someone comment that one of the cops was the others new partner. I doubted that; it was more likely someone high up the food chain decided putting a thin female in harm's way wasn't good for their career. My theory held up as I opened my door and both cops immediately dropped their hands to their weapons, gazes locked on me and their Thoughts running wild as their Minds identified my duster and the black hematite rosary dangling around my neck.

* * * *

Baked chicken quarters, homemade macaroni and cheese and steamed broccoli; Carrie's mom asked if I wanted cheese sauce on my broccoli and was surprised when I told her I preferred kosher salt only. She smiled, but it wasn't exactly a pleasant smile; I shrugged to cover up the smugness rolling behind my eyes. Thanks to Dominique I learned that kosher salt would neutralize one of the key components within the seduction potion. I thanked Lord Quick for giving me an interest in cooking and culinary as I munched on dinner; Daphne was a good cook, so I didn't have to fake being satisfied with my food: one good thing.

"He's a bit strange, Ma," Carrie chuckled. My girlfriend's approach from the rear didn't bother me; I knew where she was and knew where the potential weapons were located. **NOTHING** in her house was unknown to me by now.

Dealing with Human threats isn't new; being sociable while doing so is unnerving to say the least. I'm more comfortable prowling the Thoughtscape for mutates, hunting demon infested areas and Sanctioning scum who abuse their Psionic Gift. While Carrie's mother sauntered into the kitchen I split my attention between Following her and listening to Carrie babble about her parents. Once again I thanked Meanstreak for his intense Training; I actually looked interested and kept my gaze from zoning out while listening to Carries beautiful voice. As her mother pulled opened the cupboard I Saw her whisper silently; the lack of Psionic-based magical energy told me she wasn't Gifted, meaning the potion she'd concocted was Witch Hazel's doing as Dominique suspected and her silent words were not some incantation.

"So, young man, tell me about yourself." Carrie's mom smiled as she placed the salt shaker in front of me before sitting down. Carrie settled into her chair while sipping water from a blue-rimmed glass; her gaze darted towards me as if to say, "Be Polite." I was being *very* polite considering it Smelled like her mom was trying to get into my pants.

This wasn't my first MILF encounter; it **was** my first time being hunted by a horny older woman with access to Artifacts, and it gave me an appreciation for those stories of men who dealt with powerful, driven Females. I don't like talking about myself, and Carrie filled in some holes with information that I would rather remain private; in the end she only got what I'd carefully created: the story of a kid from backwoods Virginia who happened to have just enough intelligence to offer the chance of escape. Carrie's mother smiled and laughed at the appropriate moments, but I Sensed her growing lust cloud her Thoughts; she concealed it masterfully, adding to my belief that I wasn't the first male in this position. I just wondered if **Carrie** knew what her mother was plotting; since I don't Mind Rape with any reasonable skill, and *she* was just as anxious to jump me as her mother, I was in a position I'd never been before: cornered **Prey**.

Meanstreak told me: *There will come a time when you must Hunt alone.* This wasn't exactly what he meant. I'd Hunted alone before; not having backup gave me unexpected freedom and I completed my Hunts spectacularly, even managing to avoid the worst assaults from my Prey. This is different and I **know** it; sleeping with Carrie's mother could only destroy my relationship with Carrie... unless they were in on it together.

After dinner I offered to help clean up; Carrie excused herself: time to check her Facebook and email and Twitter - Social Management. She called it that, and her mother chided her for slipping out on her boyfriend to, "... dork out on your computer."

"He's used to it, ma. I'll be back for you in a minute, hun."

"Take your time, and tell Gracie hi for me." Carrie flashed a warning smile; apparently mom didn't know *everything* about Carrie's college social life. This gave me hope for a heartbeat until I remembered how the two females hooked up: Stoner After-Party. I helped gather the dishes and was preparing the dish water when her mother cornered me, sliding up beside me smoothly. Lust danced with playful Motherly concern simmering in her eyes as she spoke.

"So tell me: does my precious daughter still smoke marijuana?"

"That's something you need to ask her ma'am."

"Meaning she does." She chuckled softly, swishing away from me as I added the dish washing liquid. "I caught her doing it when she was sixteen. Never said anything about it since she was **very** discrete, something she gets from her father." I hummed. That settled it; smiling politely I split my Thoughts and reached out for my Brother. I needed backup.

* * * *

Brother.

Marcus!! Long time no hear!!! What's new with you?

Same shit different toilet; how ya hangin' L.J.?

Back home dealing with more useless bullshit. How's your girl... or is she an Ol' Lady now?

That's part of the reason I contacted you; I stumbled into a deep shit pile here. Carrie's mom is hitting on me... and using a Seduction Potion.

You should get up with Dom then...

Already done, but I've got the feeling my girl's scheming to get her mom stoned.

That sounds kinky...

And FEELS like I'm being set up; paranoia's kicking in big time. Mind doing me a favor and See what Carrie's thinking? She's wearing a Promise Ring I cooked up when I was back home.

You still got that thing? Thought you said you wouldn't use it.

Carrie was runnin' through my shit one day and found it; couldn't tell her about its origin, so I let her keep it. It didn't hurt that she thought I'd bought it *for* ***her.***

I'll bet; no prob Bro. Do you want a Link to her Mind?

Nope; still can't Think right with a Link active. Memory Crystal?

Done. Uh... how is she?

She'd doing well; missing *you* ***somethin' fierce, Brother. Give her a call.***

**sighs heavily* Maybe...*

Somethin' haunting ya? You Feel like Lord Quick: dark and brooding.

The Curse of Thinking too much; how deep are ya in, Marcus?

Deep enough that I've left myself several Outs; you suspect something?

Just wondering why you and I suddenly find ourselves neck deep in shit at the same time. You know the Rule: secure your Paths, Brother.

There is no such thing as Coincidence.

* * * *

The cops followed me as I entered the store. I Swept the Minds inside quickly, nearly coming to a halt when I Sensed Deke; the last time I saw the large offensive lineman was at graduation. Everyone assumes he either cheated or was graced-through; I helped tutor him in geometry, so I **know** he's more intelligent than he lets on. I also know he's a victim of Familial Association; he's got several cousins serving time for drug possession and one currently avoiding Fed charges down in North Carolina for suspicion of cocaine distribution. Deke scored a football scholarship out-of-state and managed to avoid the drug game in town by maintaining his Gentle Giant persona; his presence distracted one of the cops, a football fan, and I exploited it, Sleazing into his Mind with brutal ease. As soon as I got the information I needed I pulled free, causing him to have a headache-turning-migraine; he'd pop a few pills and things would settle down, but his concentration was completely shot for the rest of the night.

I wasn't expecting Marcus' Thoughts, but I welcomed the familiar Feel of my Blood Brother's Mind. And I wasn't completely upset that it wasn't a social call, as that would lead to us talking about Dominique. I bumped into a short, long-haired girl with massive tits and a tree-trunk for a boyfriend; he scowled at me for all of three seconds. Then he saw my rosary, and just like that the scowl shattered; he kept it in place by furrowing his brow and dropping his shoulders menacingly, but his eyes betrayed the *terror* suddenly gripping his Thoughts. I didn't know him personally, but correcting that would have to wait until later; I grabbed an Arizona green tea with ginseng and walked to the front counter. The other cop made it a point to step directly in front of my intended path, squaring his shoulders and looking over my right shoulder. So I gave him something to look at; a brunette behind me screamed as the ghostly image wavered into existence and the cop let me by, rushing towards the frightened female.

"L.J.!" Deke's thunderous bass bulldozed every other utterance. I faced him squarely and bowed slightly; he returned my Greeting properly: right hand forming a Blade's Edge perpendicular to the breastbone, the base of the palm at the bottom of the sternum. He bowed slightly, maintaining eye contact; when he lifted up his right eye twitched. I nodded, signaling that I'd call him later. The cashier made a point of avoiding eye contact as I paid for my drink: classic sign of someone who'd not-seen too much Gang activity; again I Scanned the Minds around me, this time paying close attention.

In many ways I'm worse than the cops; I tagged no less than three Bloods with Thought Markers. One was just drunk enough to start working himself up enough courage to challenge me, a member of the new gang in town: The Horde; I had my drink and was heading outside when he finally decided to whisper his intention to his boy. Sighing heavily I performed the proper *kuji-in*, implanting a vicious nightmare into his Mind. A sudden wind kicked up the sparse leaves and trash on the ground; I doubted anyone would noticed that they swirled in the opposite direction of things normally caught in the chilled-to-near-freezing breeze. I ignore the car packed with females drooling over my all-black car and its gleaming chrome accents; to them it's a sign of Money, and every single Mind inside and around the white sedan was focused on finding Mr. Money to fuck. I slid into my ride, locked the doors and was cruising back down the drag before I gave in to temptation and fried their pathetic excuses for Minds.

"Can't call Dom now, not like this." My voice was low and throaty; the soft growling breath reminded me about my last Run before returning home. Distracted by that Memory I didn't see the State Police car until it was right on my tail. I growled deep within my chest and Reached for the mind inside... slamming **hard** into the Thought Shield surrounding it.

I grinned; Thought Combat was just the release I needed, and the Wall was definitely created by a skilled opponent. I was approaching a red light, so I activated the car's Urban Escape Program; I never slowed down as I approached the intersection, the light turning green less than two heartbeats after I'd activated the program. The Stater kept pace. Seconds later I heard the expected warning warble within the Audi: the State Patrol Vehicle possessed a shielded electronic system, so using a Jabberwocky wouldn't get him off my ass. **THIS** car was rigged for catching high-tech drug runners; time to give him a bone. I Searched for a lone vehicle occupied by someone Riding Clean, finding a Mustang driven by a cute white chic bobbing to Country Music as she headed home; one small Push and she gunned her engine just as the Stater pulled up to my rear. I slowed down just enough to screw with the cop's perception, my brake lights never reacting. Sure enough the State Patrol car whipped behind the Mustang; I signaled, turned right and was down one of the many side streets. This one had a hill; the instant I knew the Stater couldn't see me I cloaked my car and Shadow Walked; the auto-pilot would return it to my house.

Well now; let's See who you are, Copper. I was slightly surprised; the State Policewoman had only the lingering afterglow of Psionic shielding around her. The **car** was heavily shielded; obviously an Artifact, I carefully prepared myself for my assault. The sheer power was nothing compared to its Focused nature. I frowned as I examined the area closely; the Wall was much smaller than it should have been. *Personalized; the closer she is to the Artifact the more complete the protection. Lover or Family member...; let's find out.* I formed the necessary *kuji-in* smoothly; the soft hiss signaled my success and a bone white snake about the size of a pencil coiled up in my right hand. I held it out at the Thought Shield; the serpent moved with blinding speed, crashing into and through the wall with ease. *Amateur or Latent despite the power; the pieces vanished instantly...*

Right then a blinding white flash caught everyone's attention, though the State Policewoman and the Mustang's driver only paused as if they'd seen something flash in the distance; I gripped Traveler as I floated backwards and to one side, avoiding most of the Psionic backlash. I didn't lose my Focus however; the Artifact itself was nothing more than a Gift... one given by a child. A ***very POWERFUL*** Artifact created by a child with enough Psionic potential that I wouldn't want to be nearby when he or she Emerged; what's really amazing is that the

Shield slowly put itself back together *without* being Infected by my serpent. **THAT** takes serious skill... more than an unskilled child could muster ***alone***; the Thought-Weave was tight and Focused. I memorized its pattern before splitting my attention.

The State Policewoman was slightly amused; Mustang actually tried the Tit-Bounce to distract her. Didn't work, but the Sex Thoughts give me all the Access I needed: the Artifact was **definitely** Tuned to her Soul. *Someone really Knows you; odd... because I didn't **SENSE** any Family Tie. Secret Lover then...*; I rifled through her Memories... jerking free of her Mind before the trap triggered.

* * * *

I didn't expect Carrie's mom to ask her about pot smoking the *instant* she returned to the living room; I didn't expect to **see** my girlfriend for at least another twenty minutes. Two surprises in less than a heartbeat; I narrowed my eyes slightly, then did my level best to erase the expression as a familiar Darkness rustled within my Soul.

"I don't mind you smoking it; I was young once. I asked because your father won't be coming home... and I didn't want you ratting me out." Carrie's jaw dropped; I sat perfectly still, one eyebrow raised; her mother smiled, and I **want** to say it was warm and pleasantly conspiratorial. I've seen that Smile before... and did not like it; Helen smiled like that before our Relationship went Down the Rabbit Hole. I knew there were Dark Thoughts churning behind those eyes; I took a deep Breath and hoped I wouldn't catch a certain Scent lurking beneath her rising Lust. "We'll just keep this as Our Little Secret."

"Wow, ma... uh... can we drink too? I mean... why do things half-assed!!" I feigned shock; my Thoughts were anything but as I Connected to L.J.'s mind...

Or **tried** to; normally instantaneous, *something* was doing its damned level best to block it. The familiar Dark Presence began taking shape within me and I swallowed my growing Fear as I tried to maintain control.

"Well... that depends on what your boyfriend says..."

There's no such thing as coincidence; I have difficulty controlling my Thoughts when drunk and my Senses become absolutely useless. Even with my Training I recognized the signs, yet didn't have the luxury of Shadow Walking through one of my escape routes... even if I trusted the extra security I'd added.

"I prefer rum if you have it." Carrie's eyes flashed; so did her mothers. I felt like Fresh Meat beneath their excited-yet-restrained gleeful gazes.

"I have just the thing. Carrie, do you remember Miss Angelina?"

"Jet-Set Angie? Sure."

"Hush!!! Well she had her son bring by a bottle of rum from her trip to New Orleans; it's **made** there. I think it's called..."

Drake's Cutlass!!! I choked down my excitement. Drake's Cutlass is aged seven years... in barrels blessed by a Mambo; I know because Lord Quick performed a Summoning and used it once. I was there... and so was L.J.; we'd earned Papa Ghede's blessings during that Run, and with my Brother being attacked I might need a bit of Papa's power, especially considering I just **knew** I was about to be mauled by a Cougar and her young cub.

"...Drake's cutlass. Have you ever had it, Marcus?"

"Once... back home."

"**OH *REALLY....*"** I grinned devilishly at Carrie; she was very interested in that Tale judging by her expression.

"I *told* you I wasn't a Saint, hun." Nowhere near...

"Well then... do you want to smoke yours or do I get my stash?"

"**YOU** have a ***STASH?!?!?!***" Her mother chuckled.

"Where did you get it?"

"Where did you get **yours?**"

"From a guy I know." Carrie rammed her fists onto her hips.

"Same here." He mother vanished into the kitchen.

"I never..."

"Like mother, like daughter." Carrie flung a small pillow at me; I caught it, thankful for her aim. It blocked her from seeing my face only for an instant, but that's **hours** for what I needed to do.

* * * *

My eyes darted from one poisoned tentacle to the next. *Nice trap; if I survive this the maker will wish they'd never been born.* I zoomed backwards, Sensing the blockade behind me as it formed. *Shit; they know enough to keep me pinned in. Who the fuck **is** this... Section 8?*

DOWN!!! I fell flat just in time; a booming explosion shattered the barrier behind me. I tucked and rolled, ending up kneeling on my left knee; Traveler was free of its sheath and the black Blade dripping vile purple ichor from the tentacle I'd severed. I Saw a mass of tentacles envelope something and grinned evilly as I prepared for what was coming.

The howl was ear-splitting; from the writhing tentacles burst long black vines with wicked thorns, some hooked and sharpened on both inside and outside curves while others were needle-like. Whatever this was it was expecting **only** me, not Marcus in full Hound mode: *Chains*. The instant I Felt the Command I was ready for the awesome Thought grenade he'd flung towards my attacker.

Where's the White Witch, Penance!! Trust a Hound to be worried about the entire Pack even in the middle of Life-and-Death Combat; strangely... he Sounded forced... as if it was taking a great deal of effort to Thought Speak.

Unsure, but I've got that covered; watch my Six while I deal with this thing.

I Smell Mundane Thoughts. So someone was **using** the policewoman's mind; I wanted to show concern, but considering I was fighting for my life... and I really don't like Cops...

I'll try to remember Chains; I focused my Thoughts as I prepared to cleave my way through the remaining tentacles. Then he was gone... and I Felt something else; something that worried me more than the unknown death-bringer I faced.

* * * *

"*HOLY SHIT!!!*" Carrie eyed the white and brilliant evergreen marijuana with naked amazement; I Smelled the pungent weed long before Daphne pulled it from its hiding place, impressed not only by the quality but its scent.

"It's called White Widow." Carrie's mom smiled softly at her daughter, gloating; she let her gaze drift my way, judging my reaction. I was impressed and let it show, though **my** approval was muted.

As a Cook I've encountered more than a few different strains of marijuana; working for Lord Quick I **know** more about the stuff than **everyone** I've ever known. As a Hound I can track lingering Thoughts, and there **is** a connection; from the hand that picked the bud to the hands bagging it for transportation... all the way down to the hands rolling up a spliff or blunt, there are lingering Thoughts, and that's all I need. I caught only **two** Scents, and the plastic bag holding the **full ounce** vibrated only one: Carrie's mom. There was also the overwhelming Scent I know as Home Grown, meaning there was either a growth of marijuana trees out in the woods somewhere or her mom had a hydroponics lab stashed in one of the three sheds I'd noticed while staring at the stars; I finalized my assessment as Hydro when I could not Scent any real earthy undertones. I sipped the room temperature rum slowly, the silent Prayer offered while Carrie poured the drinks. Unseen by their eyes, the marijuana glowed a faint Carolina blue, indicating Papa Ghede not only heard my Prayer, but offered his assistance.

"Go get comfortable, Marcus; I wanna find out where mom got her shit from!!" I smiled and reached for my glass, grateful for my girlfriend's rough dismissal. "Leave it; you remember where my room is, right?"

"I'm not trashed *yet!!*" And thanks to Dominique and Papa Ghede, the spiked drink I would return to won't leave me vulnerable; I wanted to Shadow Walk to L.J.'s side and decided against it even though I was safely in her bedroom. I did, however, contact the newbie Tech Head and had him turn off the cameras in her bedroom for at least five minutes. My Brother was fighting for his life and I had to dodge a Sex Plot; I wasn't happy or in the mood for being subtle, but that is precisely what I require now.

I'll put them on a loop; when the storm hits I'll kill the power. That way...

It'll look like a power outage; thought you said you were new to the Game?

This stuff yeah; *hacking* **is nothing new, and some of those tricks are tried, tested and true. It's the other stuff... ghosts.**

Don't antagonize it.

That's just it, how do I NOT piss it off? How do I keep it from knowing I'm there, or here, at all!!

Try a cloak program; I've gotta go. And nice work with the Avatar.

Take care of yourself Chains.

Once inside Carrie's bedroom I changed from slacks and my chocolate silk shirt into Street Casual; Carrie doesn't like seeing me in all black so she bought a jogging outfit decked out in our university's colors and made me promise to wear it when I decided to go Lounge Lizard. She even checked to make sure I **didn't** bring my all-black outfit, saying I looked too thuggish; I closed my eyes slightly, reached into the partial opening of the garment bag and Shadow Walked my hand into my closet on campus, pulling out my midnight black/blue sweat suit. Yeah... Carrie would throw a fit and ask where I'd hidden it; with the attack on L.J. and the plotting duo I would soon be stuck with, I wanted **Gear**. I can Shadow Walk and use my skills regardless of what I'm wearing, but my **GEAR** has a few added benefits. I even had a plausible excuse for stashing it away when I saw the rancid hatred in my girlfriend's eyes upon seeing me wearing the all-black attire:

"*Why did you bring that? It's new... right?*"

"Nah; old Smoking Gear... a gift from my best friend back home. Told me to break it out when I blazed with that special someone."

"You lie..." I kissed Carrie on the forehead.

The best Lie: the **TRUTH**, told with a smile on your face. I just hoped my smile wasn't... revealing.

* * * *

Lord Quick told me I shouldn't use my Gift to become an electronic Peeping Tom; after my experience in the place Marcus stayed in I figured out why. Forget seeing some wrinkled MILF wannabe doing things no porn star would do, I could actually end up alerting some ghost or damned spirit to my Presence. Spooky stuff, and normally I'd run away screaming. But I learned something from Marcus, something I don't think he intended to teach me.

Spirits crave energy, and the **source** doesn't really matter. A battery's stored energy is just as good as the energy given off simply because you're alive; I can't mask myself because of this fact, but ***can*** give them a different energy source as a distraction. At first I wanted to experiment on my own, but when a stray cat startled mom (a story for another time, **trust me!!**) I figured I'd stop by the Library for a quick glance at a few files. When I did I found myself before a **huge** metal gate and an old man leaning against a dangerously bent walking stick.

This was new; my lessons always took place in a familiar setting: a room full of floating computer touch-screens within the Library, a place Lord Quick said was tucked away inside a place he owned: Darkhaven Manor. I flashed back to the first firewall I'd experienced **as** a wall of fire, and the chuckled words Lord Quick said: *Your Mind is your greatest Ally and, more often than not, your greatest Enemy.* So I closed my eyes and tried to See the gate as Computer Code.

"Impressive attempt; **futile**, but impressive." I blinked; now there was a stone **wall** surrounding the gate, and the old man was several steps closer.

"Uh... hey there. I'm..."

"I know who you are, young one. What I do not know is why you are here; only a few Souls know of this particular Entrance into the Library." The old man's wrinkled features twitched, moving the lines as if he were thinking about many things at once.

Nothing is ever easy, especially where I'm concerned.

"I need some information; I'm on assignment." This entrance? I only knew of **one** entrance: the one Lord Quick taught me to access.

"Indeed... Then where is your pass key, Agent?" Oh shit; I never needed a pass key before. Electronic combat I knew about; **this** was something different if the withered-yet-spry looking old man's tone was *any* indication.

"Right here, Gate Keeper." I spun around, surprised by the voice and the dangerous Tone rumbling beneath the smooth words. I hadn't Sensed anyone approaching, and that meant that the speaker was *very* good at whatever he did.

He looked like a cross between a warlock, Sherlock Holmes and a **very** twisted mix-up between The Joker from Batman and one of the Killer Clowns from Outer Space... only he wasn't skinny or clown-fat. The black trench coat flared out around his legs; the black buttons glimmered as if coated by purple glitter. Occasionally it would flutter in a breeze I didn't feel or hear, and when it did the coat seemed to shimmer into a cloak lined by some softly glowing royal purple fabric; otherwise the insides were blacker-than-black.

"My apologies." I turned to face the old man and watched as he melted into nothing. And I **mean** melt; first his tattered brown coat oozed away, then the filthy, long-sleeved white tee shirt; next came the necklaces, some made from teeth. They oozed over his surprisingly muscled yet age-wrinkled flesh and drew eerie patterns on his skin.

"Quick told me you were impulsive; it never occurred to you that there'd be security measures protecting the Library?"

"Guess not..." I looked towards the visitor, leaving the verbal opening in hopes the funky-looking techno-wizard would introduce himself; instead he turned his head to one side, that lop-sided grin coming painfully close to making me laugh. I didn't because of the end-melt for the old man; his flesh darkened until it was the same blacker-than-black color lining techno-wizard's trench coat as it melted, revealing **only** a bone-white skeleton... no guts except for a purple beating heart with gleaming silver and pulsating white veins and arteries.

"You don't have an Avatar; why not?"

"Well... I've *tried* to create one, Mr..."

"Call me Ace; he never mentioned me?" I shook my head. "Then you have no idea who I am; this could be an Avatar, a construct used by another Tech Head."

"Doubt it." I squinted, examining the rest of techno-wizard's outfit carefully. Actually, I was wondering about his slacks. They could easily pass for Sunday-going-to-church standard... except I couldn't figure out what the material was; they didn't look like polyester and lacked the ordinary dull sheen of cotton. When he moved they swished slightly, reminding me of silk.

"Really? Why?"

"That outfit *attracts* attention." Especially the **loud** purple shirt and sickening green tie... which wasn't drawn tight around his neck; both had glitter in them... **moving** glitter.

"Lame... and Honest; no wonder Quick likes you. Now then... come inside; I'll show you how to unlock the gate..." *And show you where your pass key is hidden.*

* * * *

When Quick told me about the Tech Head he'd half-trained I was concerned; it's not like him to leave Training incomplete. After watching the kid's attempt to enter Silas' personal Gate I was sure of several things; first and foremost: Quick was right - the kid's a dweeb with a Heart of Gold. I almost didn't believe the Lord of Darkhaven Manor; now I do... and it makes me smile. It means there's still *something* of Nero buried beneath the layers of Anguish and ruthlessness Quick keeps tightly wrapped around his Soul; Like Tends to Like and this kid is nothing short of a White Knight, which explains one thing: how he managed to **find** this particular Gate. Only a Good Soul could ever discover the Obsidian Gate.

"Uh... Mr. Ace?"

"Just Ace."

"Oh... Ok; could you not do that?"

"What... Thought Speak? Does it bother you?"

"Only because I don't like people putting Thoughts inside my head."

"Then you should work on preventing it."

"I've tried to; Lord Quick didn't stick around long enough to teach me how to do it effectively, and he said it may take a while. He gave me a Short-Cut, but I didn't bring my Bluetooth with me."

"You really **are** inexperienced. In that case, let me give you a piece of advice about your Avatar: make one with Pockets and keep crap in 'em."

"What... like cargo pants? Don't like 'em; only swamp rats and wannabe Grunts wear them."

"Then how about a cape?"

"Like yours?"

"You don't want a cloak like mine; trust me. Now then... close your eyes and Focus on your heartbeat."

"This is looking for my pass key, right?" I nodded once. He didn't trust me and it showed in his eyes and the scrunched lips. "Can't I just... tell him what the pass key is? I mean... it's like a password, right?"

"What's your favorite programming language?"

"***HUH?!?!***"

"BASIC... Fortran... C++..."

"Those are dinosaurs!!! No one uses them..."

"Wrong; you know they're dinosaurs because someone *taught* you about them. Therefore... someone used them."

"I get it... but you're forgetting something."

"Oh really? What."

"Computers run on binary: ones and Zeroes. **THAT** is the original computer code!!" He grinned like most young wise-asses; I was beginning to like him... and see what Silas Saw.

"And no matter what *language* you use, the **code** never changes: Zeroes and Ones. The same is true for your Pass Key; anyone with enough skill can copy it, but there's a catch: only the creator possesses the correct arrangement."

"... because..."

"Because a Pass Key comes from the Soul. Now... *close your eyes and Focus!!!*"

Young and stupid, with an instinctive Trust of Good Guys and Adults; the only real Conflict I Sense within him is one that **should** be there. His father abused his mother, yet he cannot *hate* him because the scumball **is** "Dad"; good thing he doesn't know how Quick dealt with that situation, and probably why he never mentioned me. Wouldn't put it past him to have kept Meanstreak from the kid's lesson plans as well, which reminded me to let the others know: **don't** spill the beans unless absolutely necessary; the kid opened one eye and glared at me.

"You're not reading my Thoughts are you? Takin' advantage of a kid isn't nice."

My mistake: the kid ain't stupid at all; the Nice Guy with just enough Street Savvy to keep from wandering into the rough side of town. Reminded me of L.J. and Marcus... and Nero Alexander; now I *really* understood how he managed to find the Gate.

"I give you My Word; by the Honor we hold..."

"You're part of Lord Quick's ***clan?!?!*** Then you should have his Mark on you; show me."

"Careful what you wish for, Junior; ya just might get it." I let my smile fade while Focusing my Thoughts. The kid didn't have the skills to keep himself from being overwhelmed by the power the Mark of the Clan Cursed possesses and I did not want it kicking him out of the Library's system. But he asked to see the Mark... so I obliged.

* * * *

* * * *

Richard White couldn't sleep; he **knew** someone was watching him and it wasn't his mother. More frustrated than frightened the young boy flung off his covers, knelt beside his bed and prayed.

* * * *

"Momma... someone's praying."

"I should hope so sweetheart," Angie glanced at her daughter, smiling proudly until she saw the concern furrowing her teenager's brow. "Is there something wrong?"

"I'm not sure; it's like I can feel..."

Your daughter is a powerful telekinetic. Her Gift is intrinsically tied not only to her belief in God but in her belief in the Power of Prayer; I bring this up because she isn't alone in this particular Issue, and it comes with a peculiar form of Feedback.

Angie slammed on the brakes; tires squalled/screeched briefly as she gripped the steering wheel, attempting to push it into the engine block. Yet these sounds were nothing compared to her daughter's surprised, frantic scream.

* * * *

Richard halted his nightly prayer and snapped his head towards a sound he barely heard though the well insulated walls; his breathing quickened, each breath deeper and more powerful than the one before. Psionic Power hung thick in the air, cloaking the semi-dark room into oblivion silk-black nothingness.

* * * *

* * * *

I was awestruck; there was enough Power radiating from Ace's body that I Felt myself form my Big Red Button. Before I could activate it and dump my Mind back into my body I was gripped with sickening, twisting nausea; I'd Shadow Walked *somewhere*.

Keep it together, kid; I need you right now.

I did my best, though my stomach did **not** approve of the sudden movement. I tried to Focus on my Locator program... and got slammed into a big white chair; I looked around, utterly confused by my surroundings.

"Where am I?"

Command Central; I'll fill you in ***AFTER*** *you access the street cameras on Myrtle Avenue and Piney Forest Road!!*

"Uh... the CITY!?!?!? WHOA!!!!" Small white pixels glowed beneath me; they split up, each one becoming a computer screen. ***"I didn't..."***

You're in Quick's personal Command Center; figured since he trained you you'd be able to access some of his shit. Now tell me what the cops are doin'!!!! C'mon kid!!!

Before I could answer I was *thinking* the reply, screaming it actually; I was also wondering how I managed to get inside this place without accessing my Passkey **and** how he expected me to tell where the police were... and that's when small red-and-blue flashing lights appeared on the monitors. As I opened my mouth to scream, ***"ALRIGHT!! ALRIGHT!!!"*** I not only had the answer, but noticed the lights were moving in the same direction. I also sounded funny, like my voice was synthesized from my Thought Speak Voice instead of my real world tone.

"Alriiii; whoa. This thing's FAST!! There are two cars... and what's... SWAT?!?! Ace; what's going on: drug raid?"

See any DEA Ghost icons? My eyes flipped across the rapidly changing data.

"Negative."

Keep me posted, especially if any alarms go off.

"Roger that, and I wanna know just WHAT the hell's going on the first chance you get!!"

Another Reason Quick likes you: you've got enough balls to question Authority when it jerks ya around.

* * * *

I hated jerking Quick's Tech Head into the Command Center inside his old doss, but the **POWER** assaulting the wards I'd placed over his old flop-house was enormous. If the wards fell while I was inside the Library, the Feedback would cause Quick's young charge serious damage; he was better off in the command chair, and there was something about the attack I wanted to confirm.

Words of Power are fascinating things, especially those devoid of the Speech requirement. Someone cast a very powerful, highly focused Curse on the building; nasty thing, but my Wards were up to the challenge, something I'm betting the Psion caster won't like. Right on cue I Felt the negative energy gathering. I extended my Sight briefly, Focusing on L.J.; I scowled when I found him, but left him alone. Penance was neck deep in his own battle with something straight from the Chtulu Mythos and more than holding his own. This was *definitely* a carefully coordinated Psionic attack on Quick **and** his former students; the Curses pounding my wards told me they assumed **ONLY** Lord Quick placed Wards over his place. I planned on making them regret their lack of information.

Well now... I followed the energy trail to Quick's old Kitchen, a place I am **very** familiar with and have little to no love for; whoever the attacker was took the time to Bind the poltergeist within Quick's old Kitchen and unleashed a different Bound Spirit, one that wasn't too thrilled about *being* Bound.

Let's see... you go after everyone Quick knows; that means you may know about Meanstreak, but haven't run into the Killer yet. ***SO...***

When the Chains hissed the Bound Spirit immediately took notice; apparently **it** knows about Meanstreak because I Sensed its Fear clearly. When it connected to his Master... excuse me: *Mistress...* I broke her Binding Spell; before the thing could think to gloat with its new-found Freedom it howled in agonizing pain. The Psion's eyes bulged and she started choking; the Server asked her if she's OK. No dearie she's not OK; it's kinda hard to breathe with Meanstreak using one of his Chains to squeeze her esophagus until it pops, severing it while leaving no external marks: the Mark of a Master Killer. That done I checked on the new guy, materializing as a digital ghost just off his right hand side.

"Hey kid..."

The cops are heading towards a restaurant: Austin's. They JUST diverted there. Not good; someone either had a snitch inside Necropolis PD... or the local fuzz were under a Puppet Master's influence. Either option was just as viable and a Puppet Master is likely to drag Silas away from Council business; his track record with leaving such trouble makers alive is horrible, and something easily exploited. It **could** be Section 8, but they don't have full-fledged Psions on their payroll; then again... I **never** consider *any* Government Shadow-Ops Agency as having the moral fortitude to Play-By-the-Rules.

Uh... I'm hearing someone call for help; something about a State Police officer who just fell out; apparently they're having seizures.

"Listen to me carefully, Kid; things have gone to shit in a nano-tick. Contact Marcus and his friends and tell them to meet in the usual place."

Marcus may not be able to show and I have no idea... I chuckled as I extended my Sight to watch the scene at Austin's from the Thoughtscape.

"You'll get used to the Command Center soon enough; make the calls."

* * * *

OK... where's Marcus' Team? Two more monitors winked into existence. I was quickly adapting to this Think-it-Do-it style of Interfacing; when I do it I have to concentrate, or face the possibility of seeing one of my

many random Thoughts. My mom thinks I daydream too much, and I **really** don't want to hear what she'd say if I told her the truth... not that I know how to convince her that I can use my mind to access any computer. *Huh... no video; wonder...*

Access Denied. Not the first time I've seen this prompt, but it **is** the first time I've ever **FELT** the warning; chills shot up and down my spine. *OK... so how do I call...* A small green screen blinked opened just in front of my right hand; I glanced at the names, then took a closer look at the number next to L.J.'s name. *Funky; call L.J.*

***click/hiss* You must be the Tech Head Chains told me about; make it quick... pardon the pun.**

"Message from Ace: meet at the usual place with the rest of the Team. Confirm transmission, over."

Confirmed; you sound like a kid. Penance Out. *hiss/click*

And he sounded like a complete jerkwad. *Call Dominique.* **Access Denied.** *Why?*

Access restricted to Visible Presence only.

"And me without a good Avatar."

Avatar Processing requested? I remembered what Lord Quick said: *nothing is ever easy...*

After thinking about it I nodded once, sighing as I prepared for... ***something.***

"Keep the pain to a bare minimum." I saw the standardized hour glass wink on, then disappear...

* * * *

Dominique spun around, crouching slightly; both hands filled with vibrant blue energy and her eyes burned silvery gray.

"Uh... Miss Dominique?"

"An Avatar; who are you. **SPEAK!!!**" The androgynous electron blue figure took a step back while raising both hands, defending his flickering form.

"Message from Ace: Meet at the usual place!!" It... *he...* vanished as quickly as he arrived. Dominique scowled.

Prepare the House for the others, please.

* * * *

"MAN!!! Paranoid bunch...; not even sure I should call Marcus now!!" Oh well; I just hope things were going well for him.

Access Denied.

"What **now?**"

Parental Controls Activated. WONDERFUL!!! He's having sex, L.J. is in the middle of a battle and Dominique... well... *she* looked like she was **expecting** a fight!!!

I've gotta get used to how you do things, computer. Let's start with your name; what does Lord Quick call you?

Lilly-Rose.

Beautiful; are you an AI system?

According to Lord Quick: not yet. *That* made me nervous; a Human told her she wasn't Self-Aware and she believed it; to me, that means there's enough evidence to **question** his decision. That... or he lied to her/it and she/it **believed** him; Lord Quick must be a master of understatement: *nothing is ever easy...*; NO **SHIT!!!**

Where is the usual Place?

Access Denied.

Why... because I'm not an official part of the team?

Correct.

Who makes that call?

A Member of the Clan Cursed.

Great. Hey... show me my home. I wasn't surprised by the top-down satellite view; the multi-screens showing my room, the living room **and** the view which hovered my mom's bedroom door made me uncomfortable. I don't have any security cameras in my place!!!

Query: what is your level of training?

*Just above zero apparently; I **thought** I was doing well until...* Until everything became James Bond meets Cyberpunk.

Suggestion: Access the File designated Node Runner.

Ok... but what's my mom doing?

Access...

Gimme a break; is she asleep? She hasn't called the cops on me because I'm here... Another screen glowed softly; apparently I was on the sofa while the television watched me sleep!!!

THE CRASH OF LIGHTNING

From the Blackened Scroll:

On Psions and Issues

All Psions have Issues. That word may cause some laughter, yet understanding how Issues limit Psionic Gifts is vital... not only to the Psion but to any Aware individual in their life, and no Combat Specialist survives long **without** studying how Issues shape and guide Psionic Gifts and power.

It is inaccurate to term Psionic Issues as *Mental* Issues; the negative connotation is one major reason. Many Psionic Issues are tied to Belief. For example: if an Energy Projectionist *believes* their Gift is Heaven Sent they are more likely to generate what is **loosely** termed Light; this is not to be confused with the scientific term 'light' as there is, because of the limiting Issue, a Spiritual aspect. Likewise, those who believe their Gift comes from some other Source, like demonic possession or other *negative* influence, tend to produce a negative effect commonly called Darkness. In scientific terms the energy is charged either positively or negatively, possessing frequencies and sub-harmonics which resonate in very specific ways to Matter within the known Universe. Both Projectionists can destroy physical objects; the *belief* of the user dictates Positive or Negative.

The Power of Belief

Never underestimate the raw Power within Belief; it can not only Limit a Psion's Gift but on many occasions it will add to not only the power but the Focus.

Belief is a matter of Mind and Soul and cannot function without both; a word of caution: there is no need for **balance** between the two. For example: the Renaissance saw an explosion within science and reason; many wondered where Faith stood within this intellectual growth spurt. Questions posed during those Days and Nights still resonate today, and some of those questions reside within Psions. Even knowing that one's Psionic Gift is a function of genetics, there are those who firmly **believe** God granted them this ability.

* * * *

* * * *

It is selfish of me to watch over L.J. as I do; while I am responsible for training him in the Way of Shadows, I've developed a fatherly outlook where he is concerned, and that is UNDERSTANDABLY curious... and wrong. Though I lingered in the Thoughtscape, his Thoughts never far from my Senses, I wasn't following him as he cruised through the Necropolis Night. I was actually searching for a particular Mind, one which held a very specific taint on it; I was surprised he didn't Sense me as I observed him crossing the bridge headed for the main drag. Then again, he's working extra hard avoiding Thoughts of his former lover. It would be much easier if they'd parted ways because of standard high school drama; his encounters at college hardened his Heart greatly. I respect his fortitude and resilience; it takes serious Focus to confront the Hell Spawn unleashed by silly kids experimenting with a Ouija board and still have your sanity and soul in tact. For him the worst parts of his most trying mission included Shadow Walking through minds; the easiest method means falling through Sex Thoughts, and in the Bar/Club Scene at college there is no **end** of viable entry points. According to his report, the Entity headed for the most corrupt Souls, and along the way L.J. stumbled upon a child pornography ring run by a cop. He reported them to the Council and they were reported to the local authorities; the news never reported the cops involvement because L.J. fried his brain while banishing the Hell Spawn attached to his soul.

Justifiable Homicide; I remember looking at his Thought-Words while reviewing his report. I Felt his Emotions in those two words; something about that kill rattled his Soul beyond simple Feedback from a dying Mind/Soul. Section 8 spent over one full month inserting the lies necessary to cover up Psion involvement, which probably explains why they're tailing him around Necropolis. After all: ***The Council does not get involved in Mundane matters***. Technically L.J. **is** Mundane. His training allows him access to some Psionic talents, but on the genetic level the tall, pale young man isn't a Psion. Not that Section 8 gives a shit; he has the Skills, and as far as they're concerned that makes him **our** responsibility. Once they discovered who'd trained him, their paranoia went through the roof. I'm known from *obliterating* the rules and have ***absolutely*** no love for Assassins; the now dead Law Enforcement member may have spared his young daughter from his sickening actions, but I wouldn't put that beyond any possible future plans. He controlled the distribution of that filth and paid well to ensure the safety of the King Pin's servers; the guy the news claims was the leader just had more of the stuff in his possession than anyone else. L.J. didn't pursue the King Pin, and I agree with his reason; hunting Human, Mundane scum leaves a Soul Taint that never leaves.

I don't have his worry; after taking vengeance on Jeanie's ex-husband for murdering my beloved and my unborn son, my Soul is about as foul as any demons. I don't dwell on my actions, and I accept the unbridled Hate her teenage daughter has for me. She knows I'm a Psion and Voudoun, and believes I had a hand in her father's suicide, the Excuse Section 8 crafted to cover up Psionic involvement. There's enough Hate in her that I Watched to see if she'd take it out on her old boyfriend, **L.J.**; I still worry she'll carry the grudge and harm him. My students have a great deal on their hands and the future will only see this burden drastically increase; so every now and again I cruise through the Thoughtscape's Necropolis echo in search of her Mind. The return of the College Freshmen is an excellent time, and she has plenty of White Noise to cover her reappearance, not to mention enough exposure to my Power that she might have lingering Resonance after-effects. I avoid the known Trap

Spots; she didn't use drugs before moving out and I doubted she had the connections in town. Imagine my surprise when I Heard a drunk, stoned dingbat mention her name; I Moved towards the drugged mind, stopping short when I Saw where it was located.

I didn't enter the building for many excuses; nothing prevents entry physically or limits my Gift... I do not enjoy the Scars or their memory. By profession I'm a Cook; that place and many of the people still working there did their damn level best to destroy my love of the Kitchen. I have a few friends there: Keys and Melodie sprung to mind and for a brief instant I allowed a smile to flit across my taunt lips. They reminded me that not everyone and everything about Necropolis conspired to crush the beleaguered guy wringing those tainted waters and terrifying Thoughts from Flesh and Soul; they offered kindness and compassion, and for that I am eternally grateful. They are not the only good Memories I snatched from that place; I actually chuckled when recalling Christian, my Blood Brother and Packmate. I haven't spoken to him much, and I blame myself and the responsibilities the Council placed upon my life.

The resident poltergeist lifted its slightly bulging eyes towards me, recognition flaring within its black/red orbs. I bowed respectfully as I Sensed the dingbat mention Gina once more. She's calling my Love's daughter, and I Saw images of partying and handsome males staggering through her alcohol addled Mind. I ignored those and Watched as the invisible data stream connected the smart phones, betraying Gina's location quickly. I was not overly surprised that she was with Jeanie's parents, but the Psionic defenses surrounding the place did surprise me: they were not the remnants of my former setup, but consisted of new, haphazardly constructed walls. I prepared for the onslaught ahead before my visit, grimacing as I found myself expecting Death.

* * * *

"Hello Gina."

"Silas." Unadulterated, rancid Hate filled her voice; she wasn't surprised by my sudden appearance within her sanctuary however. I should have been concerned, but fatalism and my own uncaring Nature simply wouldn't allow me the luxury. "Why are you here? Come to obliterate the last trace of my Father's bloodline." My gaze drifted from Gina to the picture of her mother resting prominently on her dresser; part of me wanted to die right there: they look so similar.

"Why; is that what you want me to do?"

"*I **WANT** my Family back!!!* You took **EVERYTHING** from me!!!"

"That's a lie and you know it; your father killed Jeanie in retaliation for rejecting him." I found myself wishing there was Anger in my Tone and Voice; instead there was only the coldly brutal Truth I often use when speaking to someone I cherish greatly. And for this Sin I found myself looking over my shoulder for God's swift Judgment.

"Which would never have happened if **YOU'D** never entered our lives!!"

Hate is an interesting Emotion; it always clouds the Mind. Gina's Thoughts weren't Hate-clouded; the muddled smoke swirled in and out of her Thoughts too evenly, and Hate's glaring Red was nowhere near as bright as it should have been considering she blamed me for the deaths of her mother and father. This was fascinating and troubling.

"Not even I have the Power to tell the Future, Gina."

"But you could have..." Now **that** was Anger, raw and white-hot; it jammed in her throat forcing her words to slam into its white-hot dam. The thing *soothing* her anger wasn't cool-white or Logic gray. I spoke as I observed the coffee-stain brown/Pepto Pink entity carefully as her Anger removed its Cloak, taking careful notes of how it behaved.

"We cannot help who we fall in Love with, though often we want to, Gina. I love your mother even now."

"**THEN WHY DID YOU LET HER DIE!!!!!!**" The sickening influence pulled away from her Mind as Anger once more claimed her blazingly beautiful Mind; free of the thing's influence Hate seized complete control over the young woman. She swung at me wildly; I grabbed both arms by her wrists, blocking her kicks easily without needing to resort to *Koppokoshi*. It's easy to say I only saw Hate within her eyes, but it is also a lie; Love, my Great Foe and the thing Denied me by God Almighty Himself roared behind her flashing eyes. Love for those forever lost to her: her arrogant, demanding father and...

It is important that I say this: Gina's mind conjured up Jeanie's wondrous, wonderfully amazing image; her Thoughts called to her mother's spirit. The skin and hair on my neck crawled; I wanted to run away... was terrified that Heaven's Light would sear my flesh if my Beloved were allowed to venture from that blessed place. Yet... another part of me shook with rabid anticipation. It wasn't the hope of Seeing Jeanie again that had me near-slavering; it ***begged*** God to obliterate everything I was because of what I'd done. Gina deserved her revenge and I'd earned my damnation long before that Moment. At that Moment all I **Desired...** was the oblivion Nothing granted: to cease being a Thought even within **God's** Mind and Heart and Soul.

"I have only Excuses to offer; if they will help you grieve I'll tell you a few Lies. But make no mistake: I am not God, nor do I have the power to stave off Death." I have great Power, but my greatest ability is also my greatest Curse: I Spoke honestly. Gina burned her Hatred into my eyes, though it was nothing compared to looking into hers: she has her mother's eyes. Pain ripped at my Soul, reopening Wounds and leaving them to bleed freely once more; yet I remained stoically cruel, appearing cold and distant as I struggled to look sympathetic, caring... **Human**. And with this came the maniacal Truth: God would not grant me Oblivion... would not lock me away within Nothing... not yet.

"I hope you burn in hell!!!" Gina hissed; she jerked her arms and I released her.

"If that's the worst torment I suffer, then Thank You for the blessing." I stepped back into the Thoughtscape, leaving my Love's daughter to her hate... and the Presence twisting her to its Will. And there were no tears in my eyes... despite being saddened that God apparently decided to let me live one more moment. There was only infinite Cold as I instinctively used my Gift to leave a silent Watcher, tasked to monitor the thing violating Gina's Mind.

* * * *

Watching yourself sleep is creepy.

"So... HEY!!!"

Awareness alters voice patterns; incoming transmission.

"From?"

Marcus; connection made and secure.

"How'd you get into the Command Center, kid?"

"Ace..."

"Shit; how bad is it?"

"You're supposed to gather your team and meet at the usual place; the others got the message already. Damn computer wouldn't let me contact you."

"Say *Please* and she might give in, pardon the pun; thanks for the head's up."

"Are you alright? You sound funny."

"Just a bit tipsy and high; nothing unusual."

"If you say so, Chains..."

"What do you hear?"

"Well... it sounds like something's missing. I can't put my finger on it, but there's something missing in your voice." And don't ask me **how** I noticed, since I had no clue **WHAT** was missing; I only knew that something wasn't in his voice... and it worried me.

* * * *

From the Blackened Scroll

Tech Heads are Empaths whose ability is closely linked to complex machines. **Cybermancers** are Tech Heads, though they are limited to computers; do not mistake this Limitation for a weakness. Consider just how many complex machines possess microprocessors or use GPS; a Cybermancer has access to any computer-controlled system. This makes them somewhat limited, as a pure Tech Head can operate a Model-T where a Cybermancer cannot. A Tech Head with a love for Steam Punk may even be capable of operating a steam engine vehicle; to a Cybermancer such a vehicle is literally off limits.

These distinctions blur, however, when considering Thought Crystals. Remember: microprocessors are *currently* made using silicon ***crystals***; in theory, this gives Cybermancers an edge when dealing with Thought Crystals. In practice, there is a very major difference: **THOUGHTS**. Computers process data but cannot ***CURRENTLY*** Think; by their nature, technologies using Thought Crystals do not *Think*, but are created by Thinking creatures and powered by Thought energy stored within crystals. As such, they are prone to several side-effects; the most common side-effect is one many today consider superstitious: the Machine with a Soul. Tech Heads state this side-effect thusly:

Given the constant clash between the Thoughts stored within the crystal or crystals, it is inevitable for certain clashes to spark something similar to Intelligence; rarely, this clash generates what can best be described as the intelligence of a lower life form or that possessed by Spirits created from life forms.

Thus we have a curious confluence; there are many tales of the *Ghost in the Machine* and in every case it is of a non-sentient computer becoming sentient to some degree; this is what can and has happened within machines equipped with Thought Crystals.

* * * *

He's right. As we stood outside and watched snow trickle from the heavens I tried Contacting L.J.; our Link was active, but he never replied. Whatever occupied his attention had to be worth his full Focus; that not only spells major trouble, but if it kept **him** occupied then the chances of my current situation getting messy jumped, and I couldn't rely on my best friend and partner for back up.

But I did have the new kid...

Hey... you there?

Online; what's up?

See if there's a mind reader program in the Command Center's database.

Apparently so, but I don't have access to it.

Did you ask politely?

Yes. Now it's telling me the program is Mission Critical; what's that mean? I closed my eyes, and tried to catch a snowflake on my tongue.

WHOA!!! I'm in... did you feed it a password or something? And How? Ok... got... huh...

Got what?

The program's name: Mind Link. It requires two Minds.

So? Link mine to my girlfriend...

No.

Why not?!?!?

Someone tried to breech our connection just now... and it looks like it came from your end; you're not secure, Chains.

Keep me posted Cypher.

* * * *

"Cypher... I like it!!"

Recognize designate: Cypher.

Lemme see the breech attempt again; something didn't look right about the cyber attack. As I replayed my conversation with Chains I came to the moment when the computer sensed the attack. *Freeze it; can you tell me what kind of program's being used?* I was surprised to actually **finish** my Thought, and worried when it took a full three heartbeats before I got an answer.

There was no attack program.

Then what... no...; it was a ***WHO...*** *Someone like me.*

Incorrect; Thought signature does not comply with known Cybermancy frequencies. Cybermancer, eh?

Real fast: are Cybermancers different from Techno-Wizards? I mean...

Affirmative.

Check known Tech Wizard Thought frequencies then. While the computer ground away at that I flicked my eyes towards my sleeping body... just in time to see my mother creeping up quietly to turn off the television. *If she wakes me, will I lose everything?* Not good...

Affirmative; Secondary Response activated.

* * * *

"Calvin? Cal honey..."

Her son mumbled incoherently, rolling over to face the sofa's back. She smiled, stroking his dark brown hair tenderly.

"Get to bed soon... and remember to take out the garbage in the morning." He raised one arm, the hand flopping at the wrist as if to brush her away... or direct some chaotic orchestra. She kissed him lovingly on his temple, tucked him into his favorite blue and gold blanket with silver shooting stars...

* * * *

"I remember that tune; Gammaw used to sing it to me when I visited for the Summer." Mom hummed the tune as she walked away, and I couldn't stop the smile or flood of memories... not that I wanted to. It reminded me of better... more **NORMAL** days and nights.

Negative Techno Wizard/Cybermancer signature detected.

"So... if it wasn't either of those, was it HUMAN... and *alive?!?!*"

Source was not ethereal.

Now **this** was a computer function I could like; *so... no Ghosts then.* I frowned, suddenly wishing I had a glass of cranberry juice cocktail and some sugar cookies; Thinking was becoming difficult.

"Don't reply; I'm talking to myself."

When nothing happened I closed my eyes and tried to remember the last song I'd heard on the radio; while I did that I kept asking myself how to connect Chains to his girlfriend without leaving him wide open to another attack. I could record her Thoughts if I had a big enough hard drive but...

Is it possible to record Thoughts and Memories?

Affirmative.

Where... no hard drive is big enough; what's the storage medium?

Thought crystals. I opened my eyes; on my left was what appeared to be an inventory list.

How many will I need to record his girl's Thoughts for tonight?

One Category B Thought Crystal should suffice for Audio/Visual.

Get three ready, and monitor Chains' location for signs of the Psion who attacked our connection.

Incorrect; the attack did not come from a Psion.

Hold on; you said it was Human... not a ghost. That means Psion, right?

Incorrect; continued analysis eliminates all known Free Talents from viable suspect pool.

Still Human though... right? No Reply. None.

RIGHT?!?!?!? I only heard silence from the Command Prompt; I swallowed hard.

Nothing is ever easy...

RAGE OF SHADOWS

From the Blackened Scroll:

The Thoughtscape and Denizens

The Thoughtscape is constructed of Thought energy; this gives it several fascinating and nearly unbelievable properties. What is known about the Thoughtscape is highly limited, but there are several parallels to our universe, heretofore called the Prime Universe. The Thoughtscape is inhabited by native flora and fauna; the more intelligent creatures are called **Denizens**. What is known about Denizens is this: they tend to be formed primarily from one Thought or Emotion; this is important to know and understand as it leads to a better understanding of how the Denizen will behave.

Another parallel is seen in how Denizens breed. Denizens do engage in sexual practices, yet these practices seem to stem from the nature of the formative Thoughts; for example:

Denizens formed from Human Thoughts and Emotions tend to mimic Human mating rituals and styles. What makes this particular example of importance is best seen in the Human Thoughts of lower life forms, such as bacteria, viruses, fish and insects and so on. To a large degree, the more intelligent the Thought the more it controls Denizen behavior and breeding; yet it must be stressed that this is not always the case. There are certain Thoughts which morph together in ways which create awe-inspiring, often terrifying Denizens.

If there is a point of contention it is this: Denizens don't *die*; they can disperse over time or be dispersed, but actually **die...** that has not been observed. What has been observed is this: once Dispersed, certain slivers of the Denizen will incorporate other Thought energies and reform. These reformed neo-Denizens are called **Mutates**.

* * * *

There are several dark sides to Denizens and Mutates. Denizens are formed from Thoughts and Emotions; no one in the Prime Universe will argue that there are Evil Thoughts, though they will debate what is ***considered*** evil. So it comes as no surprise that some Denizens are best described as Demons or other fantastic, even magical, creatures. What must be understood about such Denizens is more warning than raw Knowledge: ***they are bound by certain rules, such as the need to be Summoned in order to manifest within the Prime Universe or any other universe... EXCEPT THEIR NATIVE UNIVERSE.*** This one rule is responsible for the Thoughtscape being considered a gateway to Hell, and indeed, it **can** serve as such a gateway.

* * * *

* * * *

I've fought demons, ghosts and Denizens; the thing I tangled with wasn't any of those things and that alone made it dangerous. It was worse. It **knew** me. I moved fluidly, swinging Traveler with calm efficiency despite the thing's obvious knowledge of how I reacted, and I began questioning Marcus' Sense; this was **NOT** a Mundane creation. It wasn't a Mutate either, and I'd encountered a second generation Mutate; this thing... was something new, and it drew its power from the State Policewoman's mind. The logical thing to do, then, was kill the cop; logical and easy: how I prefer things. Like I said: the thing knew me... *well*; so I forced myself to calm down and think things through.

The technique is one I learned from one of the scrolls Lord Quick keeps hidden in Darkhaven Manor's underground storage vault. When the tentacles attacked again I was ready, and suddenly the State policewoman and the Mustang's driver were hit by the thing **in the Real Universe**. Only the mustang's driver reacted, knocked clear across the road; that's when I saw something I didn't expect: Artifact energy.

Section 8; why am I not surprised. The tentacle passed through the cop without harming her, but in doing so revealed more than it obviously wanted about its nature; as it passed through the policewoman the other tentacles wrapped around her Mind recoiled slightly. *So... you don't like for your host to experience physical Pain...* I moved swiftly to one side, yet I remained squarely Focused on the abomination; it anticipated my movement and several tentacles lashed out. I sliced them easily, yet where I previously avoided the parts I dropped them into the Real World, opening Shadow Gates beneath them as they flailed. This seemed to confuse the entity as it quickly reconstituted its losses, which vanished in a putrid looking puff once dumped into the Real World; good... and it didn't appear to *learn* from my new tactics... **even better**.

The cop went rigid; the entity's tentacles jerked wildly. While focused on my movements and the Shadow Gates they missed the Gate opened at the bottom of the cop's taser as well as a small opening over the trigger mechanism; while she tried to figure out what was going on, her hand, thanks to her training, went for her sidearm: a perfectly natural movement the entity wouldn't take too much notice of while not only revealing the flesh beneath her arm pit, but drenching it in **natural** shadow. And like a well-trained officer of the Law, she'd moved the other arm as well, giving me a direct electrical path across her heart. I expected her to go rigid; I did not expect the voltage to cause current flow within the entity; even the pieces burned as electricity flowed through them, which was really interesting.

I didn't get the chance to examine things closely however; another Artifact was activated, this one tasked with containment. It was probably very precise, but it didn't work; one of the severed tentacles exploded within the Real Word and I used the Shadows it generated to escape. Normally I'd leave an eyeball behind to observe what happened next; with Section 8 involved I had a fairly good idea: Clean-Up, and there's only one place I know of that offers any hope of security when they start scouring Minds: the Cursed Grounds of Darkhaven Manor.

* * * *

I wasn't surprised by what I Saw; there were two black sedans parked in a cut-off and both were empty. Section 8 **must** be desperate if they sent such a small force into the grounds surrounding Darkhaven Manor. I moved silently towards the entrance, manifesting in the shadow of a large, twisted maple tree. I heard leaves rustling to my right: a Psi-wolf probably, judging by the way the wind seemed to hesitate before shifting the overhead branches. I waited until it revealed itself; two large yellow and black orbs appeared, the colors swirling and churning calmly as the massive body materialized.

Welcome Young One; your path is clear.

What of the intruders?

They struggle, but make their way steadily; they wield stones protecting them from Human spirits, but the Pack is unaffected. They Sense no ill will from them.

Thank you for the warning, Lone Hunter. Are they armed? Lone Hunter chuckled.

They wield Human Killers with silver long-darts; your Species relies too much on legend.

So they were *expecting* werewolves? That spelled trouble; yet Lone Hunter said he Sensed no ill will from them. Odd? Not if Section 8 were **prepared** for Psi-wolves; and if **that** were true, the agents wouldn't be armed with silver bullets. There had to be a new player in the game... working **with** Section 8, but not an Agent; forget trouble... this was terrifying.

Lead me to them, and tell the pack to fall back. I followed Lone Hunter as he darted through the shadows; an eerie howl shattered the night as he called to the Pack. Ravens cawed as we ran through their territory: **beware the Humans**; something about the intruders worried the murder of ravens. That was good enough for me; when Lone Hunter slowed I took time to Summon an Ally.

"You called, Penance?"

Thank you for coming Sarlek; I may have need of your skill and sharp mind.

"You have no idea; I expected your Summons when I noticed you doing battle with the Ancient." I was surprised he knew what the thing was, but not by his knowledge of my predicament; Ally Denizens are like Spirits in that they do not like being Bound by... or in Sarlek's case... **to** living beings. ***"How may I assist you this night?"***

The humans up ahead have several Artifacts in their possession; what are they?

"One wears a pendant; it keeps Human Spirits at bay. Are ALL Humans so blind, Penance? The pendant's Creator firmly believes in fate; there are small fairies and a few pixies swarming around them."

Really? That doesn't sound like someone from Section 8; they'd want NO ethereal energy near them. Of course... that would be like throwing up a thermonuclear flare inside the grounds...

"Indeed. The other... is a threat."

How so? The Pack...

"Has never encountered this; do you recall our discussion about Playing with Forces one does not fully comprehend?"

Yeah...?

"This Human is prepared to deal with Legendary Threats: werewolves and Vampires..."

Now THAT sounds like a Section 8 Rookie.

"You've fought a vampire before..."

He was a Psion, remember?

"And you remember how he became one of the so-called Eternal Dead."

I do; he was bitten by an older lover who believed he was a vampire. The guy's Mind was so twisted by vampire lore that his Emergence ended up being Limited by his belief in the viral origins of vampirism. ***Your point, Sarlek?***

"He gave blood before his Emergence." Oh shit: Resonance; because it was his blood, it expressed the psionic energies.

Where is his blood now...

"Flowing through the veins of the one wielding silver..." Wonderful; and because he worked for Section 8, I'll lay good money he's a Test Subject. Which made the unknown Player someone I **definitely** wanted information about... and fast.

Can you take control over his body?

"Easily, Penance."

Good. Lone Hunter will you help?

Of course Young One; if they threaten my Home I am Honor bound to remove their taint from the land.

* * * *

L.J. crept through the Shadows; his Thoughts mirrored the Autumn chill as he stalked the government agents.

"We're being followed..."

"Get ready; I figure the wolves will make their move soon."

"Good." The six-foot-plus man scanned the black night for the reds and yellows which betray living creatures while slowing his heartbeat until it appeared to stop completely.

"This way." He tried to follow his companion but his legs would not move; he tried to call out, but nothing happened. Neither heard L.J. as he appeared from the Shadow of a pine tree. "You coming?" The smaller, well-built man turned to face his partner.

"He's busy; who are you?" Before he could answer something heavy slammed into his back, knocking him to the ground. *"Stay down or die: your choice."*

* * * *

You move like breath Young One; it is an Honor to Hunt with you.

Thank you, Lone Hunter.

"What of this one?"

Take him to the Abyss; I'll meet you there after this one tells me what he knows.

"Why not just take the information from his mind?"

There may be a trap waiting for anyone who tries; not really in the Mood for another battle with one of those things.

"Ruthless AND wise; you ARE growing up, Penance. I will be at the Abyss waiting."

With the Soul Prison AND its cargo in tact, Sarlek...

"Of course."

I motioned for Lone Hunter to vanish; I removed the metallic necklace from the agent's neck and secured him to the ground by Shadow Art.

"Struggle if you want; you're mine until I say otherwise. Why are you here?" Silence. "Ok. When you wanna talk I'll be here. But I'd hurry if I were you; zombies love fresh meat and can sense it from miles away." The Section 8 agent chuckled; he spat out a few crumpled leaves before speaking, and his voice was **packed** with Governmental arrogance.

"If I were you I'd release us now; the Government doesn't take..."

"Shut the fuck up; you're from Section 8, one of the Governments Black Ops agencies... and **they** can't see you here. Satellites can't see through the barrier, and anyone looking will only see another stretch of Night-kissed Virginia backwoods. Now... before those zombies get... too late." I went silent; I Smelled the undead carcasses before I heard their shuffling forms. The agent started hyperventilating when one groaned; though some distance away I drew the sound close enough to inspire the restrained agent's immediate compliance.

"And the thing is... I can make it so you feel everything when they tear into your flesh."

"I'll die..."

"Only if I let you." He went silent at my bluff-threat.

"You're Meanstreak," he whispered, completely horrified. I knew Meanstreak's reputation well and didn't answer; the agent struggled desperately, almost digging a trench with his chin before grim reality drained his muscles.

"Finished? You're weak..."

"What do you want, killer."

"If I repeat myself..." I growled my words; he exhaled, admitting his position wasn't favorable.

"We're here to make contact with Silas Quick."

"He's not in the city." The agent laughed.

"Not Meanstreak... gggrrkkk" I tightened the Shadow restraint around his neck.

"You doubt me? Silas isn't in the city."

"Then... who was... with... his... s... stepdaughter..."

GINA?!?!?!

"One of your agents perhaps," I snarled/growled.

"Be careful, L.J...." The Voice didn't surprise me; the instant I blasted my old friend's name into the Thoughtscape I knew Dominique would show up.

"I... I..."

"He can't breathe; if you won't Mind Rape him you'll have to let him breathe."

Stay back Dom; this scum might be wired.

"Glad to see you too."

* * * *

Are you sure Cypher?

As sure as I can be; the attack didn't register as Psionic. I checked it myself; there's SOMETHING *humanoid* ***there, but I can't find it. Chains... you'd better get outta there; this is WAY over my head. Ain't getting' paid enough for this...***

Wanna bet? Quick doesn't leave the Clan without some money stashed around. How's the link to my girlfriend coming?

Here's the password for her link; I set up another for her mother. Whatever's going on, I'm in this until the end, Chains.

Or your mom flips out; you're young.

Speaking from experience?

Naturally; what's the word on the others?

According to this they're on the Grounds; got any clue where the Grounds are? Chains chuckles softly...and darkly.

They're fine Cypher; tell 'em I'll be there as soon as I handle my Biz. Chains out.

I really like the new kid; I can Sense the Goodness within him even through the improvised Thought Speech. I did **not** like his report; there was something *similar* to a Psion either in Carrie's house or roaming the woods. Added to Witch Hazel's seduction potion, her addressing me as *Hound*, and now... Carrie's odd behavior: I was **definitely** in trouble. So much for turning the tables and ending up in a seriously kinky three-way with mom and daughter; this was looking more and more like Dazzle, Divide and Conquer.

Carrie's mom was the first one to head back inside, driven by the deepening cold she claimed. Carrie was next, scampering inside when her smart-phone beeped; I told her I would be inside shortly... then sparked up another joint. She shook her head, laughing softly as she ducked inside.

Cypher. I chuckled when I Heard the *click* as he connected.

What's up Chains?

The link... there's a delay.

From my Scrubber; I don't trust the Thought Crystal to block any virus code, and it takes a shitload of processing to scrub the data clean.

Use another Thought Crystal.

When I'm sure the code is golden; right now I'm manually filtering it through several stages...

Peeping Tom?

Nope; this computer won't let me see what she sees or translate her Thoughts into a document file.

Drop the firewall or scrubber or whatever you're using; I need the speed.

If you want, but I wish you'd think it over. Another click and Cypher was gone; so was the nagging delay. I took a long, slow micro-drag while I rummaged through my girlfriend's mind haphazardly.

* * * *

"The attack... when did it happen? What was I doing?"

Designate-Cypher was looking at Mind Link.

"And... when did you Sense the attack?"

Fifteen nano-seconds after you formulated the program's name as Thought.

"That's no coincidence; who knows about Mind Link?"

* * * *

Chains; there's a possibility that Section 8 is involved. Super-secret Government spooks are bad news.

Thanks; do a satellite search for heat and Artifact signatures at my location.

On it n...; shit. Chains... **there's a squad of heat signatures at the edge of the woods there, and according to this...**

A shitload of artifacts; understood.

What can I do from here?

Not much... unless you wanna do a favor for a paranoid brotha.

Name it.

Check Carrie's father; Witch Hazel said she worked a little magic to keep him from showing up. I wanna know what that magic was, and if she had to do a damn thing at all.

I'm on it, but you need immediate evac...

Hounds don't run blindly; get to work and watch your Six, Cypher.

* * * *

I relaxed the Shadow around his throat; the Section 8 agent gasped for blessed air, his fingers finally relaxing and losing their frantic near-death twitching.

"Speak; there's not much time." The moaning grew louder, accompanied by the slow, steady shuffle as they struggled towards fresh meat.

"D... don't... *please!!!*"

"Then answer my question."

"We didn't find the girl at her home; so we were sent here to see if she'd made it to the Manor."

"And they only sent two agents; liar."

"Look... I ***swear!!!***" I tightened my Grip around his neck

"He's telling the truth L.J." Dominique; I was surprised that I didn't Sense her assault on his Mind. I was also surprised to Sense her *controlling* the undead, keeping them from going into a feeding frenzy. What I thought were simple animated corpses left on patrol nearby were Psi-Zombies... those foolish people who wandered into the grounds surrounding Darkhaven Manor and met Death in one manner or another. Most of them were cops or Government spooks who'd stumbled across Section 8 somehow; that Dominique held them under her control with enough skill to hide her Actions/Spells from my Senses said much... and none of it I liked.

*Stay out of their Minds, Dom; I ran into something new earlier... and I think it's something Section 8's experimenting with. At least I **HOPE** it is.*

"He's Leaking; Fear won't allow him to cloud his Thoughts. Apparently his partner has...; he claims to be a vampire. Silas said..."

Ok... call off the zombies and keep him strapped to the ground; I'm going to interrogate the other one. Back shortly; we'll talk.

"I'll hold you to that; be careful."

Always. Before leaving I adjusted the Shadow restraint around his neck... and let him hear chains clinking softly; the reinforcement of my supposed identity squashed his subtle attempts to test his restraints. I nodded grimly and continued to the Manor, my Thoughts racing wildly as I struggled to keep Emotion from clouding my judgment... judgment I knew I would desperately need.

* * * *

I made sure Dominique couldn't Sense me: I Shadow Walked on top of Darkhaven Manor's roof where the Manor's four invisible dragons guard the larger-than-reality-allows building. Dominique and I have fought against and with dragons; she isn't too fond of them... and I can't feel Dragon-Fear. I wasn't surprised the broad, clear back yard was obscured by tall trees; unless there was a reason otherwise, the Manor concealed everything, so there was no yard and no sign of the back house Dominique, Marcus and I often occupied. The deck attached to Lord Quick's room yawned beneath me, speckled by tree limb shadows; where the tool shed should have been stood a *tall* grove of bamboo trees. Multi-colored orbs winked off and on, darting between the bamboo leaves and tree trunks. I could just make out the land's curvature by the sweeping lines of tree tops, but knew enough about the Manor to not make assumptions.

*Need breathing room that bad? She must **really** love you.*

I choked down my surprise at Lord Quick's deep Thought-tone; I expected him to admonish me for my lack of focus, so his quiet, even Thought-breath was a welcome surprise. I didn't turn around; it would be pointless. Though it sounded like he was behind me and to the right I knew there was only empty air at that location; I didn't think Lord Quick could fly, so that meant he was Projecting or tucked away in the Thoughtscape.

You have a choice: open your Heart to her or become like me... an emotionless sack of shit driven by Honor. And it ***will*** *happen that way; war does something to the Soul.*

War? What war... and what does Gina have to do with this?

I leave that for you to discover.

Why? You know we used to date...

And I will always Love her mother; even so, I am a ruthless bastard and will not spare her or be gentle. I'll tear her Soul apart if she's hiding something, damn how it makes me Feel.

Bullshit; you didn't Banish her mother's spirit...

Only because it was her Final Wish before Moving On, Penance. Had she not Begged Properly I would have ignored her.

Banishing the soul of the Woman you Love?!?! What kind of Monster are you?

They call me: Man. *Now before you make your decision, consider my take; you'll NEED that heartless, utterly unfeeling part of you.*

What's going on Silas...

It's about time you address me by my first name; you're not a kid any more... and you are not my Student. Take responsibility for your actions. Think shit through. And no matter what else happens, never turn your back on those who Love you... even if they tear out your Heart.

It was a mutual thing. Silence; guess Silas doesn't buy my bullshit either. Dominique and I parted ways because we were going to different colleges; I told myself it was for the best... that I'd be there if she needed me. But the second I got my first solo assignment I threw myself into it; didn't take long before I was all about school and Shadow Work. The beautiful, wildly powerful Witch I'd once done battle with, and now called Friend, was part of my Past; and for the first time... I admitted the Truth: **I was running!!** Running from my Past... and headlong into insane, bizarre adventures.

Every now and again her Mind reaches out for the connection between you; it always encounters the Last Wall. I Know that Sound better than you ***should****.*

I know... Again silence yawned between us.

You think Gina's involved; how?

Not sure, but the goon Dom's watching said you stopped by to see her.

I did, but there was no one around.

Not even in the Thoughtscape?

Well now; so that's what that was.

What?

Something was feeding off the Hate and Rage within her; without knowing what it was I left it alone.

Thought you were a heartless bastard; that sounds like something you do when you care.

Perhaps; had it attacked me I'd already decided to behead her.

You're so full of shit...

On my Word of Honor, L.J.: had the thing attacked me I would have killed my beloved's only living heir.

I believed him, but not because of his words; there wasn't a shred of Humanity within their Tone. I know he lost his first born child when Gina's mother, Jeanie, died, but there was something else in his Thought-tone; it sounded like Meanstreak's inhuman, utterly emotionless Voice, yet not as unforgiving or ruthlessly sadistic.

You took revenge, didn't you.

Yes. The emptiness in that one word chilled me to the core; it wasn't cold because **that** would be *something.* If Silas thought I was close to becoming just like him...; I let my eyes drift skyward until my vision included the pale crescent moon.

The other agent; is he a vampire?

Not in the purest term; from studying him he's only been recently infected with something posing as leech-blood.

Sarlek said...

I know... and he is correct... technically; while there was a blood transfusion, there's also some very skilled Surgery involved.

Section 8's EXPERIMENTING on its own agents?!?!?

You sound appalled; that's good. You also sound surprised; why? There are many within the Government who make their living turning even the most benign things into Weapons. And they won't listen to Hollywood Fiction; they honestly believe they ***can*** *control such terrifying weapons, damn what the History of nuclear weapons teaches.*

Is this why you trained us...

It may feel better if I say yes, but I never Lie to those I care for; I prepared you and Marcus to deal with the amazing changes coming to Humanity. There is no one set purpose to my actions other than that.

Guardians of Humanity...

No: Guardians of Sanity; Humanity has enough self-imposed, self-righteous guardians, most of whom are in it for the Power and Money. Now... go deal with the other Agent...

Before Sarlek gets bored! I couldn't help but chuckle; Silas gruffed/snorted one as well. I dropped my head as I looked behind me reflexively. ***What do I do about Dom?***

Never ask a sociopath with a penchant for being brutally Honest about Matters of the Heart, L.J.; you ***won't*** *like the answers and despise the advice.*

Thanks, Lord Quick. Oh... before I go... the new kid?

Cypher. He's got a few issues, but I like him. Treat him like Family, L.J.

Copy that... Old Man; watch yourself.

Shadows Guard you and yours, Penance.

THE HOWLING WINDS

Incoming transmission; Designate - Penance.

Hello Cypher. Unlike Marcus, L.J.'s voice had no hint of digital processing. It also had none of its previous asshole quality, though why I noticed this I don't know.

"Hey there!! Glad to hear from you L.J.; you made it to the meet in one piece."

There's been a delay; how's Marcus doing?

"Not sure; I told him he needed to get outta there before... whatever or **whoever** it is... makes it move."

Hounds don't run away from Danger.

"Yeah... he said something like that. Look... I've been tracking his girlfriend's father, but he's being hid.

Something is actually **blocking** my attempts to get a lock on his location."

Another Tech Head?

"Maybe; if so then they've got me out-classed by miles. I'm *still* tryin' ta figure out how **this** computer works."

Command Center is only for the Elite; and before you ask... the fact that it hasn't spit you back into your body means you've got the stamina to hold out. Just don't be surprised when you return to your body and feel like shit. Still... get some rest as soon as we're safely on the grounds. I'll post guards near your house.

"Copy that." L.J. smiled as his image faded; it was the first time I'd seen him and I almost laughed at this refined Avatar. The sides of his head were shaved bald, and he wore the top in a pony-tail slicked back with mousse or something. Still... the cloak he wore reminded me of the ones Star Wars Jedi wore, and his face was a dead-wringer for Alan Rickman: Professor Severus Snape; it was an odd Avatar, but the end result was that L.J. appeared firmly in control of the situation. The only flaw was his eyes; they showed deep compassion and bright humor.

He's got a slick Avatar. Ok... back to Marcus and the search for his girl's dad. I was at it for several minutes before Marcus contacted me.

* * * *

I connected to Daphne's Thought Crystal briefly; everyone was back inside and I was rolling up another fatty, feigning Weed Head thoughtfulness as I mentally inspected the crystal. Carrie was stoned, a goofy, lazy grin fluttering over her entire face. Her mom was watching the Weather Channel, completely oblivious to everything around her; as soon as I started reviewing her current Thoughts I changed my opinion: *she was ignoring Carrie!!!* Why? Flipping through Daphne's most recent Thoughts I spotted an image of her dosing Carrie's macaroni with something; it's the only reason I even attempted viewing both Thought Crystals at the same time. I was Feelin' Nice and surprised when I managed to keep my Thoughts Focused on **one** Thought Crystal; that should have been my first clue to what would happen.

Then I Touched both crystals. *What the...?* The hairs on my arm stood on end; my heartbeat quickened, pounding my chest with each *lub-dub*. I Know what Human Thought Looks and Feels like, and the... *thing...* before me wasn't Human; Deep within my Mind I heard chains rattle, startled by the vile Presence I observed winding around both female's lustful Thoughts. I blinked, stunned by the realization that I'd seen it in both Female's Minds *and* within their stored Thoughts darting through my High; then Understanding reached the Place where the chains hissed angrily... and a part of me I'd thought long and forever dormant... woke up.

* * * *

Hey Cypher... can you connect me to L.J.? I need to find out what this... ***thing*** *looks like to the Mind's Eye.*

"I've got a translation program online... gimme a sec. HEY!!!"

What... ***you've seen something like it before?!?!?***

"ME? No... but apparently the computer **here** has."

Access Denied... Access Denied...

Sounds like something Lord Quick doesn't want you seeing. Hey... what was...

"Another attack; checking... Who are the Council?"

Why... are they behind this attack?

"Must be; I'm just sitting here watching some killer code fly around. Which Crystal did the image come from?"

My girlfriend and her mother... when I connected to them simultaneously; why?

"There's something in the image... no... wait: Data! I'll treat it like any other data packet... **THERE!!** There's another set of instructions... virus?"

Where... inside her Thoughts!

"Yeah. Mind Control from another Psion, maybe; Marcus... you **NEED** to get out of there. I'm contacting L.J. and asking if he knows how to get in touch with Lord Quick..."

You See it? I wasn't sure about much, but when a Big Red Button with ***Emergency*** appears before you during a time of need... you can either take a chance that it's a trap or try to jam the thing into whatever console it's attached to; Option B, please.

* * * *

Greetings Marcus.

Lord Quick... what is this?

Coffee-stain brown/Pepto Pink; I studied the Memory carefully before answering, keeping my tone even despite the growing Dark Thoughts rapidly filling my mind.

I've only encountered it once, and still have no clue. The Council believes it is a threat, and I tend to agree.

It's wormed its way into the thoughts of my girlfriend and her mother.

And its growth is slowed by the sleeping potion her mother administered, not to mention the White Widow in her system; of course... it ***helps*** *that it was grown by a Latent Psion.*

Who... her mom?

No... Female though...

Her Aunt; this is getting too complicated.

And with the snow storm shifting into high gear you're gonna be stuck there until they both pass out, and that might prove difficult.

Sir?

Her mother's Sex Drive may be slowed some, but she's still counting down until you feel the full effects of her potion. You have less than thirty minutes before she figures out you aren't enthralled; ideas?

Not off hand, Sir; this is where I'd ask L.J. for something.

And where he'd find a way into her Thoughts; so... I offer you this: she's never been with another Dom.

I can't go back Lord Quick... I won't.

Very well; try this then. You'll have to tear the paper and re-roll; you can say its from a small stash you forgot. I left the powerful marijuana strain in his right front pocket and exited his Thoughts carefully... though not without Implanting a carefully worded Thought-Bomb within his Mind.

* * * *

I hear you have a Name now.

Lord Quick? SAY!!! Alright... would ***someone*** *tell me why I keep switching voices?*

You are within a small pocket of the Thoughtscape within Darkhaven Manor; I took the liberty of bringing your physical form here... after it trudged into your bedroom that is.

You took control over my body!!!

No; your mother told you to go to bed; you've made that particular walk half-asleep before and your muscles Remember the way. All your body needed was the Mental Command from you, and faking **that** is easy: you hear you mother in your dreams telling you to go to bed...

And the body does the rest; and because I've already heard her ***say*** *that...*

You comprehend things quickly; it will save you and the Team, maybe soon.

Why... what's happening?

That thing you saw...

DIDN'T see; the computer wouldn't let me.

Because I knew you weren't ready for it; as things stand, you'll have to **get** ready. I will warn you now: when you wake up you'll have a headache; you'll also know things which may cause you to question your sanity... among other things.

* * * *

"Please: call me Daphne." I smiled my best Playa smile as my girlfriend's mother dragged her fingers over my arms, she looked into my eyes, searching for confirmation of her potion's hold over my senses. I hummed low and deep, nearly growling; I returned her caress, using techniques I swore to never use again on a Female. "I must say: that's some good weed you have, Marcus."

"Thank you, Daphne." I purred the words into her ear, modulating my Voice just enough to accentuate the Psionic-high from the AK-97 that Lord Quick Shadow Walked from his personal **collection**. Mundane marijuana will get you high; Psion-grown marijuana contains buckyballs: fullerenes. When properly used an Empath can insert subliminal programming into these buckyballs; blazing up will get you high and a shitload more. Meanstreak taught me how to place Thoughts within these microscopic orbs, though **he** wasn't at all polite about the Thoughts inserted. I didn't have enough time to check the Thought program Lord Quick installed, and really didn't **want** to know, if his earlier suggestion was any indication.

"I guess my daughter was more tired from the drive up than she let on; pity." ***Lying cunt.***

I chuckled softly, some lame excuse mumbled incoherently as I rammed Blacksoul back into his hole. When I first began my Training I'd get so blasted horny it was pathetic; without a girlfriend or fuck buddy I had no real outlet, and jacking-off only made things worse. Found a cure for it: Helen; there was just one catch. After using my skills, whether in training or on an assignment, the Sex Thoughts fed off of the Psionic energy generated; I could dump this excess energy into someone, **so long as I had sex with them!!** Helen was... was a MILF; she had a high sex drive and I was her first teenage lover and Black lover. She seduced me, as much as any female can seduce a kid who drools over her while she sunbathes in her back yard; when I finally approached her I discovered she Resonates with the energies radiating from my young Mind and Body... not that I cared. I thought she had a thing for me... that I'd gotten lucky; I could learn about sex **and** deal with this nagging bullshit my new-found powers brought. It never occurred to me that something might go wrong; by the time I knew something wasn't right I'd turned Helen into an addict. Sounds like bullshit you hear from every swinging Dick and Playa runnin' the Streets: *She's addicted to my dick yo!!* It wasn't my dick or the sex or anything physical: I'd dump the blackened Sexual over-Thoughts into her during our sex sessions; that energy... and the twisted bliss it brought her, hooked her worse than cocaine and crack combined. Soon after I realized that, I realized **I** was just as hooked to dumping my emotional baggage into her Mind. I managed to regain control, but not before putting Helen into a coma; she died six months later, and I swore to keep that side of me carefully locked away: **Blacksoul the Unforgiving.**

Daphne sauntered by me, rubbing her body against mine; I Felt Blacksoul's savage smile tug at my lips as Memories of Helen screamed within my head. I followed her movements as she slithered up next to me; her ass swayed gracefully... ***like a true Slut.*** I inhaled deeply, ignoring the fact that Daphne was probably enjoying my struggle. Her Seduction Potion wasn't the problem; if I allowed my Mind to wander I knew where it would end up: the Images of Carrie as I tucked her in for the night. I avoided looking at them in the Thought Crystal; Blacksoul kept flicking his gaze towards the images and each time those cold silver-black orbs fell on my girlfriend I Felt wave after wave of white-hot Lust, each wave topped by frothing, churning Darkness. ***You should See what you already Know; come...***

I sighed, flopping down onto the sofa; I really **like** marijuana, but AK-97 and *most* psi-breeds erode weed's natural beauty. The subliminal programming wasn't designed for my Thoughts, but can adapt quickly; the same thing would happen to Carrie if she smoked some, though she wouldn't experience Blacksoul if I maintained control, and that was not looking likely with Daphne turning things up **WAY** past ten. ***Come... see what your lover thinks; gaze upon her dreams...***

"Care for another drink?"

"Got single-malt Scotch?"

"Sophisticated!" ***She purrs nicely; will she scream...***

"Every now and then I get the taste in my mouth..." ***That's it: babble on and on; lure her closer...***

That's the worst part of dealing with Blacksoul: it knows Females; of course it gains its knowledge by Mind Rape and has absolutely no remorse for the damage it leaves behind. Carrie says I'm too nice at times; she may be right, but there's a **damned** good reason. Until this evening I never Heard Blacksoul's vile, nearly demonic, throaty hiss directed towards anyone, especially her; I was actually beginning to hope I'd managed to conquer its sadistic, unrepentant evil. Maybe... *just maybe...* I was learning how to trust... how to Love...

You know the Dangers of that cursed Emotion; if you need a reminder... come look at your beloved as she dreams about you. OR...

Daphne slid down beside me, snuggling into my arms; ***a harlot... there's no shame in her Thoughts.*** I hate agreeing with Blacksoul, but the way she purred/hummed as she breathed in my cologne had me thinking along the same lines. I needed space and took it, but not before lazily running my index finger over her shoulder. It was pure instinct, done because there was an attractive, horny Female pressed against my body; Blacksoul inhaled, pleased with my natural reaction and honed skill.

"Drinks?" I forced Stoner-mirth into my tone after a close-mouth cough, scraping Blacksoul's cold ruthlessness from that one word.

"Hmm? OH!" Daphne giggled/tittered/chuckled; she rolled her hand onto my chest, each finger stroking the smooth fabric of my hoodie with just enough pressure. ***She's GOOD; and you?*** As she got up that same hand crept towards my crotch, swinging away *just in time* for an *'accidental'* seductive dick-stroke; she had one hand on each thigh, bending over to display her full breasts.

"A True Predator has survived being Prey." Meanstreak's sepulcher flat tone echoed through my Mind. I wasn't looking directly into Daphne's eyes, but I Noticed the predatory steely glare instantly. Blacksoul growled softly as Power swirled within my Thoughts; Darkfyre streaked through the infinite Darkness as lightning through storm clouds. ***She smells Victory***; I Smelled the unmistakable joy of a Predator certain of the Kill. My gaze darted to Daphne's freezing her in place... while I shattered the Walls surrounding her Mind with one savage burst of Thought energy.

* * * *

The Abyss exists outside of Space-Time as Humans know it; some scientists are actually aware of it, though they have a different Name for it: *Outside of the Known Universe.* They also have no real concept of its size, shape or vastness; thanks to a previous Assignment I know enough to know this: the Abyss is at least as wide as several universes and beyond infinitely bottomless. Before the Universe winked into existence there was something else in that particular Place, maybe Nothing: a prison designed by God Almighty; the universe's creation left a massive chasm between what was and the Reality we know today, though to hear Silas tell the tale, Nothing simply curved around Reality, never even noticing the creation at all. Sarlek paced some distance from the edge of the Abyss, the first energy from the universe's creation crackling over the flowing obsidian fur covering his body.

Sarlek? I don't hear...

He was annoying me; Humans scream at the slightest Pain.

Keep him chained, I will speak with him. The Section 8 Agent appeared as if someone squeezed an inflatable doll from the Soul Crystal; instantly the non-air filled with an ear-splitting, tortured screech/howl as he thrashed wildly. I waited until the sound creaked into labored undead breathing, then spoke without compassion.

What is Section 8 doing? You were sent to Darkhaven Manor with a Purpose.

What... WHAT HAVE YOU DONE TO ME!!!!!!!!!!!

Nothing I cannot undo; answer me, or I'll have my associate toss you into the Abyss.... eventually.

I'll tear out your throat and bathe in your blood.

His Mind is shattered; you will have to completely destroy it if you wish to get information quickly. The agent whipped its head around hissing at Sarlek... who smiled beneath the marble and wood Mask. ***I welcome your attempt, Human; it has been FAR too long since I've bathed in the blood of the truly foolish.***

He isn't Human... not quite; they experimented on you... CHANGED what you were. What did you gain in return? Power? Money.

More than you'll ever know. I See you now; you are the one called Penance. The figure shuddered as I poured raw pain into its scattered Thoughts; that's when I saw it.

By the Void; what is that abomination?

Something new; it's not a Mutate or I'd Know. Apparently it doesn't like electricity very much... White-hot and electric blue lightening belched from the mouth opening in Sarlek's mask.

Interesting; now this thing's screams make sense. Sarlek bent his head to his right shoulder; I didn't need to see his face to know the quizzical expression dancing on his twisted features.

Talk. What were you doing stumbling through the grounds surrounding Darkhaven Manor? The howls became plaintive; the Agent tried to claw at his flesh, but neither arms nor fingers obeyed his rapidly deteriorating Mind. I watched as the foreign Influence whipped about wildly, smashing Thought fragments as if they were thin, frail glass. Sarlek chuckled joyously, increasing the fury and randomness of his electrical assault; I watched carefully, waiting for my Moment. One white/blue bolt arced between the agent's eyes; he threw his head back, and I Saw the influence pull free of his Mind completely. Before it was clear of his flesh I slapped my hands together, both index fingers and thumbs touching while interlacing the other fingers. Darkfyre ripped through the distance, piercing the Influence squarely, driving it towards the Abyss' unknowable depths.

Impressive; he's alive. Well done Penance; you showed great power and even greater control. You've grown stronger in this scant moment you call Time. The ancient Denizen will never give me credit for showing restraint, and for it... control is **not** the same as restraint; it would help if he **believed** in *showing* restraint when dealing with an enemy. Besides... something worried me.

Get clear of the Abyss, Sarlek; something... I Felt the powerful energies before large cracks tore into the Abyss' surface. Sarlek vanished, reappearing on my left and slightly behind me. He wasn't afraid; Sarlek has no real concept of Fear. He was impressed... and **that** said a shitload about the entity, none of it good.

By the Unholy... that abomination is trying to break OUT of the Abyss!!! What...

Ask later; gimme the Soul Crystal and fade, Sarlek. He handed me the baseball-sized Artifact and returned to his corner of the Thoughtscape. I withdrew the instant after I crammed the Section 8 Agent back into his unearthly prison, Crafting a Hidden Eye to keep watch on the Abyss; I tasked it to dump the images into a Thought Crystal, one I'd buried in the woods outside of campus. Whatever this thing was I didn't want it anywhere **near** Darkhaven Manor. Not until I knew what it was and how it had the strength to even *attempt* an escape from the Abyss.

Gina...; frowning, I darted through the Thoughtscape, checking my rear constantly just in case something or someone was following me. If something like that was inside her Mind I wanted to know exactly what it was... and how to stop it.

* * * *

The instant the Agents moved towards the house where Marcus struggled to control his Inner Demon I obliterated their Artifacts; someone didn't instruct their creators properly: that many Artifacts in such close proximity is **not** a good thing. Some were tasked with preventing Marcus from Sensing the two eight person squads while others attempted to cloak **all** Psionic emanations from Artifact. One thing their tactics betrayed: they know Marcus **isn't** a true Psion; if his Inner Demon, Blacksoul, remained quietly Chained deep within his Mind they might have been successful. Unfortunately for them their plan virtually guaranteed Blacksoul's reappearance: they used an older Woman to seduce him; they had no idea what he went through with Helen, and unless Meanstreak's student has grown compassionate, the white carpet of Daphne's home will run red with blood and gore.

I Heard one Agent mentally scream my name; another immediately tried to Focus their mind into a Search Light, scanning the immediate area within the Thoughtscape. It fell upon a Shadow, and instantly another agent jumped into the Thoughtscape. He wore black combat gear, and I smiled; the head gear reminded me of the gear worn by video-game black ops personnel. I Heard the gears whir as he lifted his MP5; when he returned to Reality his fellow agents gasped. One went rigid, shocked by the sudden spray of blood covering them as the lifeless, **headless** body jerked with spasms on its way to the ground.

They were not dealing with a highly skilled Mundane; I am Lord Silas Quick, Member of the Council. I am bound by Council Rules, but when there is a Threat to **any** Psion I have a tendency to break and redefine those rules. The Council does not get involved in Mundane matters; this is clearly a Mundane matter, but Mundanes abusing the knowledge and wisdom shared freely by the Council... **makes** it a Council Matter. As one of the curators of Psion

Lore and History I take personal offense to Section 8's violation of ancient teachings and blatant disregard of wise warnings.

And I haven't even gotten to the most selfish excuse: Section 8 was targeting **me** by targeting my former Students. I watched as several agents reach for Artifacts, the search growing frantic as realization punches holes through the Hope swirling within their frail frames. Someone tried to contact Headquarters; they made a mistake in putting **all** communications on one agent's shoulders, especially considering the person's neck rests beneath the shadow of a tree branch. It didn't take much more Chaos; suddenly well-trained mil-spec operatives were little more than frightened children eager for mommy to turn on the lights. Except for one: he charged forward, heading for the house Marcus and the others occupied; unlike him I was not hindered by the blowing snow. So I waited for him to get close enough that his shadow slipped up the wall; another agent caught sight of this and their muscles geared up for their run. He was at a full run when the other agent spun around, placing his back against the wall... only to realize his terrible mistake; before he could grab the flash-bang I vacuumed out his entrails, dumping the contents behind the other running agent with a loud sickening gush/plorp/plop. Running Agent slid to a halt, his gaze locked on the dying idiot's jerking form; when I finished I let his corpse fall, the entire lower back missing, exposed to the bitter cold along with the cleaned body cavity.

And... **no screams**. Oh they screamed as they died; I made sure they felt every agonizing moment, and they **definitely** screamed... perhaps even prayed; Sound is nothing more than a different energy form and I dumped this energy into the Screaming River, a particularly frightening location within the Thoughtscape. I must say: no one surrendered - honorable; of course I didn't give them a *chance* to surrender, so there's always that. I kept two alive only because the infestation in their Thoughts remained somewhat cohesive; one went to Council Surgeons who were *too* eager in my opinion. Then again... I kept the other one to torture; I started by Stripping him of certain Memories since he'd never see his unborn child or wife again. After that, I simply induced Pain; it doesn't matter what the nerve or neural pathway is *designed* to transport: Pleasure, Pain, Temperature... I Forced it to transmit **only** Pain. Too much pain and the brain naturally shuts down: a Survival Instinct; **I didn't let it.** The infestation *tried* to kill its host; I didn't let it. And I was fascinated that it would try killing him *instead* of escaping; self-preservation may not be within its programming and **that** is something worth knowing. Or... it **can** survive if its host perishes; this is also valuable information.

The infestation moved frantically, severing neural connections anywhere it could reach; I kept it active, pushing its limits and Recording everything. I Heard the Agent's Thought-scream: ***MAKE IT STOP!!!!!!*** The infestation didn't reply to his mental command or the anguish; it stepped up attempts to kill its host, eventually pulling free of its place within the Agent's mind. One short blast of Darkfyre knocked it clear of the Agent; properly separated I tossed the half-dead human frame to one side, though I didn't ignore him completely. As he crumpled to the ground I Forced his Consciousness into a Soul Crystal; at the same time I surrounded the infestation in a sphere of raw electricity.

Before you die I'll tear what I need from your Mind; because I'm trying this whole Mercy concept I figured I'd let you watch.

PLEASE!!!! Don't... I...

Yeah... there is that; incoherent babbling is a side-effect. Still... if your Will is strong enough, you ***might*** *be able to Focus long enough to Speak. Meanwhile...*

Within the electrical orb the infestation cowered, and that isn't an egotistical statement; wave after wave of naked Fear radiated from the orb's center, so I briefly connected two points through the interior. It failed to avoid the crooked bolt; the screech/scream/wail sounded pathetic during the contact and even more so afterwards.

Sympathy; were I someone else you might get it. Speaking of which... do you want to die now... or after I've torn your mind to pieces. Zombie-like, the trapped consciousness Focused on one Thought: his Wife Angelica, caressing her pregnant belly. He was strong-willed... and she was very beautiful. Their Child was truly blessed to have such loving parents. Pity.

* * * *

Somewhere inside my Soul I Understood: she wasn't Helen; somewhere inside my Heart I begged for forgiveness, but stopped short of calling His Name. Daphne saw only what I allowed, and I did not allow Remorse or self-pity to weaken my steady Player's Gaze. When the lights flickered neither of us broke the hypnotic, lust-bloated moment; only the loud bang as the circuit breaker tripped forced any change, and Daphne blinked. What took barely one-half heartbeat was more than enough time for Blacksoul and I to become One. Though the entire place was dropped into utter darkness, I saw perfectly; I Heard her triumphant Thoughts ringing in her ears and did not sneer. Knowing the rough Shape of her Thoughts as I Know and Feel my heart beating within my chest brought only cruel, savage, emotionless ruthlessness; it felt Proper, the impenetrable darkness covering everything.

Marcus!!! The things inside their minds don't like electricity!! This time I allowed my lips the sadistic smirk as the Thought Voice popped/exploded within my mind; I chuckled, touching my Tone with subtle nervousness while slowly moving my right hand towards Daphne's temple. Just a touch, a simple laughable moment masked skillfully, appearing to be a lover's lustful advance as static electricity leaps from my fingertips into her temple;

though she will only remember a brief flash of light and her own mildly surprised annoyance, the thing violating her Mind jerked violently as Pain and electricity surged through it. I'd Guided the current through her brain expertly, destroying only those brain cells already assaulted by alcohol; one tentacle positioned itself perfectly, leaving a Shadow across itself. Before it could react I ripped the Barrier asunder, forcing the darkest depths of the Thoughtscape to engulf it completely. Only her swooning body prevented me from Shadow Walking after my Prey; then again... **there was Prey here as well!!!!!**

* * * *

Cypher; drop your Link to Marcus; this is a Battle he must face alone.

Understood Lord Quick.

I used to think Government Agents had a crappy job; doing morally questionable things because someone in a suit and tie sitting in a comfy chair decided, "It's necessary.": sucks. Now **I'm** the guy doing morally questionable things, and I don't even have the comfort of saying, "It's above my pay grade." I'm here because... *because I wanted to know and now...* ***I KNOW TOO MUCH.***

Lord Quick? Why did you teach me? I mean... why am I here?

You're here because I asked; I suspect you're trying to ask if I chose you for some specific Reason. The Answer is yes, though I doubt you'll ever believe it.

Try me...

You can still laugh. During your Down-Time you play video games, and within your Thoughts is an Image of your Mother that Burns brightly; you still find pleasure in playing football and other sports, and thrill at the wonder of going on your first date. You are eager to learn how to drive and look forward to your vehicular freedom with wide-eyed innocence you honestly cannot appreciate... but I do. Of your own volition you open the door for others; you Respect your Elders and know full well Respect is ***earned****, not simply given. And above and beyond all of these... you are still utterly fascinated by the Thought of True Love. Put simply, Cypher: you're still Human. The others have been places and done things which make them question this, and for that I take full responsibility. They are still young however, and that grants them the ability and Strength and perseverance to overcome the teaching of one twisted Soul; if you have a purpose... it is to remind them not only of their Humanity, but Why I chose* ***them...*** *and you.*

Which is...?

To Protect the Future. Great; no pressure THERE.

* * * *

I stood before the large, heavy oak doors of Darkhaven Manor for several long minutes; my Thoughts lingered on both former girlfriends despite my best efforts to clear my Mind. I knew enough to not Shadow Walk inside the main building, especially during a crisis situation; there are too many dangers lurking within the Thoughtscape in its immediate area, some ancient beyond Time itself. Even so, it was the only place I knew that had the answers I sought; and in order to do that...

"I seek Solace."

Enter and find what you Seek, Child of Mortal Shadow and Light; welcome to Darkhaven Manor. No sound greeted my ears as both doors opened; nor was there the usual sight of the large chandelier glistening before my eyes. Instead only mournful darkness awaited; I bowed low and respectfully before entering, keeping my gaze locked on the yawning portal as long as possible and quickly refocusing it the first instant I Sensed the vastness beyond.

Black beyond oblivion engulfed me as I passed the threshold; even my Senses were blind, though I knew there were things observing me. I'd walked the Trail of Sorrows before, so I knew **some** of the formless masses darting through the Darkness. My Thoughts churned incessantly as I made my way to the first of the red and obsidian Pillars of Nothingness; I ignored the sudden, silent wind's low, haunting howl/moan and gave the Forgotten Guardians only a brief nod as I walked by their invisible forms. Each saluted, a soft rattle from their sleeping Blades acknowledging my passage through their domain. Far down the path lay my destination; I made my way without Feeling or Thought of the dangers I'd recently survived: they were one in a long string, one I expected would only get longer. Though there was only darkness beneath my feet, I heard and felt compacted dirt beneath my boots as I strode with boldness I didn't really Feel. Soon I found myself within a vast chamber, my image reflected faintly in the black-marble floors; before me the Throne of Bones rested on a dais crafted from Human skulls. Two gleaming steel-silver braziers glowed on either side, both held aloft by iron stands with dragon's talons for feet. The deep purple seat was unoccupied, though two shadows peeled from the impossible shadows behind the immense bone structure.

"He is not here, Penance. There is somewhere else he must be now."

"A treasured Family member Passed On; it's best he be alone to Think on matters."

"I have need of his Knowledge and Wisdom, Alexander."

"And so... we are here; what troubles you so much that you ask the Manor for Solace?" Alexander Charles Edwards, Ace, waved one had over the shadow covering his features; I expected to see the white kabuki-style Joker face, but was greeted instead by a black-and-white harlequin half-mask. Instead of splitting his skull vertically the designs went from upper left to lower right, and the dividing line: a soft, semi-metallic green and softer, glowing purple undulated.

"Gina. What's happening to her?"

"He endeavors to find that very Answer, Shadow."

"I sent that... thing... into the Abyss."

"We know; it tore its way free after you left." I frowned. "Do not worry; I saw to its eradication." Meanstreak's hollow tone held his customary savage glee after a battle he considered worthy of his skill.

"My thanks, Master of Chains; forgive me for leaving a mess for you to clean up."

"There is nothing to forgive; it was a difficult Foe, one Worthy of Death by my Hands." It wasn't the first time I'd heard Pride in his voice, but it was the first time *joy* tickled his normally emotionless baritone; its presence did not ease my mind one bit.

"If that's true... I've gotta get to..."

"No you don't; Silas doesn't want you there right now. You're needed at Marcus' side; he managed to confine one of them, but another rests within his girlfriend's mind... and he's Gone Under."

"Family First."

"Gina is Family." I believed the Words, but they did not ease the creeping pain I knew would soon consume me. Gina left us because of what happened between her mother and Silas; she expected him to protect Jeanie... always. When her mother was killed by her father Gina's world exploded. Then **he** died... ***mysteriously***; I had a clue what happened, and it didn't require Psionic Gift. One Thought, remembering my conversation with Lord Quick, told the story.

"Then choose, Shadow; do as Lord Quick has done on countless occasions and Choose who will see you at their Side during their most difficult Moments."

"You, Penance, are chosen to Lead." Ace turned his hooded head towards the throne's bare purple lining. My eyes wide, I knew what wasn't said. One day, I would have to take my place upon the Throne of Bones. One day soon, **I** would Lead and others would Follow; I was eighteen, yet at that moment I Felt instantly aged, a shriveled Old Man gazing down through decades of choices, mistakes and regrets. And utterly, completely alone; I felt my tone age and deepen as the burdens before me slowly coalesced within my Soul.

"And Dominique? How is she?" Somehow I kept her name from lodging beneath my Adam's Apple; it made me feel... disgusted with myself. I noticed that my efforts met with Meanstreak's approval; his slight nod pissed me off, but I understood the unspoken Thoughts with agonizing clarity. I was acting like any good Leader should.

"Growing rather impatient waiting on you; she hasn't left the grounds since her arrival. I fear something happened between her and her mother." I sighed heavily.

"The Burden you imagine is less than a Summer's breeze compared to the Reality you have... and the unknown additions lurking in the Future, Shadow."

"Then... her mother's infected with one of those things as well? How wide-spread is this?" I almost kicked myself for asking when I saw the look on Ace's face.

"The Council is busy debating that." Meaning Lord Quick was busy **doing** just that... while figuring out how to deal with the loss of someone he cares for. I nodded slowly, coldly aware of why he'd trained Marcus and me. The Council may well have other assets working on the problem, but only Lord Silas Quick possessed the skill to deal with a sudden assault and return alive.

"I cannot Sense the Connection with my Brother; it's like... it comes and goes... like a radio signal does when you're driving through the mountains or something."

"Something Silas attributes to this thing's growing power; he planted a Command within someone nearby. It should allow you access to her Mind, though when you Shadow Walk..."

"Sex." I swallowed hard; the last time Marcus was Under it took both Dominique and I an entire month to pull him from the pit of depression Helen's death visited upon his life. Since then he's gotten much better I think, though he avoids *anything* even remotely considered Rough Sex; makes me wonder what happens when... **IF...** he Thinks about Making Love.

"You still have that hang-up; there's hope for you yet. Now go... help Marcus Remember." I nodded, turned and took one step; something about Ace's words bothered me. I was well on my way to my Brother's side when it hit me: ***he was CONCERNED!!!!*** That shouldn't bother me; it **should** make me feel a bit better in fact. It didn't; that it didn't *really* bothered me.

Am I becoming like Lord Quick: an emotionless bastard? I shoved my rambling Thoughts into a dark hole, where I would hopefully deal with them... after I dealt with everything else.

THE PRICE OF THE FUTURE

I gazed upon my cousin's body from deep within the Thoughtscape. Normally I would consider it little more than an empty shell; I found it impossible to do that, not when she was one of the few Souls offering Prayers for my safety and comfort during those dark Days and Nights so soon after losing Jeanie. She was there when I returned to Necropolis after losing everything to Hurricane Katrina, one of the few I recognized as truly one of God's Children. Like some Dark Protector I watched the doctors and nurses move with practiced, solemn care as they removed monitor leads and carefully tended to her lifeless frame. For once I am grateful for the control over my Gift; I didn't smell the sickening, sanitized, Death-bloated stench within the hospital. I also didn't hear her parent's torturous cries; only their Thoughts bore witness to my Presence, and they quickly winged their way past my hovering Shade. Behind and above me

I Felt her Spirit, joyous and full of Light; though my eyes faced forward, observing the doctors as they pronounced her dead, I Saw her Spirit clearly, clad in Eternal White and radiant beyond measure. I thought on the Words I never said, especially, "Thank you." When I Needed someone willing to spare the briefest Moment to Pray for my Soul, she was there; we never talked much, but the Bond was... **IS...** Strong and Eternal.

Didn't excuse my selfish actions at all, and it didn't make her loss any less painful. I envy her now; held by God's eternal Grace and Love she no longer Knows the constant grinding suffering and burdensome Doubt that plagues The Living. So... I returned her kindness: I Prayed... for the first time in years.

Lord on High, I know you seldom heed the Words of a truly Damned, especially one you seem to enjoy tormenting. I know she rests within Your powerful arms; I know she will never again Know Pain or suffering. All I ask is that You touch those she left behind... especially her Children. Because I did not spare Jeanie this Thought I doubt You will hear me, but if another Prays along the same lines, Send her golden Soul to offer them Comfort and Solace; the World You've given Humanity is in turmoil, and if I am correct, under siege from without and within. Keep her Safe. Keep Safe those she loved, for I go now to do what I can... Knowing I cannot do but so much...

In Your Name I Pray... I beg; Amen.

I turned my Sight away and moved rapidly through the Thoughtscape. Eventually it settled upon a familiar form: Melodie; my brow furrowed as a recent Memory bubbled from Dark depths. There is, within my Existence, no Light without Darkness.

* * * *

"Gonna stand Superman-style while she blows ya?"

"Is that what I'm supposed to do, Ace?"

"Askin' the wrong schlub; I could care less."

Same here; like most breathing Males I enjoyed having a pair of soft lips wrapped around my dick, draining stress and semen. Yet each time I looked down I found my Thoughts were frozen tundra beneath endless, star-barren skies... when they aren't soaked with blood-red, emotionless Madness.

"Think she's got Skillz?" I shrugged.

"You don't care?!?! What's up Quick?"

"Dancin'."

That is, I kept hiding the soft, sad-sack schmuck Melodie searched for within my eyes and posture; when necessary I am an excellent Liar, though it always leaves a foul, fetid Taste on my tongue.

"She's thinking about Jeanie: wondering if **you're** still hung up on her."

"Jeanie is dead old friend; her Memory fades fast." See?

"And you don't sound half-dead with Anger; normally that means you've found someone else... but ***NORMAL*** ain't your way." I shrugged, adding a faintly amused smile/smirk/grimace as Melodie pulled one of her many Tricks from memory.

"I'm Thinking. Actually trying to figure out Why I haven't Mind Raped her yet."

"Morals?" One corner of my lips lifted into a full smirk as I snorted a soft chuckle; I covered the Truth easily, running my fingers through Melodie's hair and taking a deep, measured breath. Her eyes smiled, though why I Noticed this is perplexing.

"Nope, and I can't even say I'm being Respectful. It Feels... like making a simple choice. Ones and Zeroes; Code."

"You're looking for Humanity within your Thoughts and Actions again; won't find it and you know it. So... why keep looking?"

"No real clue. When's the last time you talked to Angie?"

"Earlier this Summer; she's concerned about you." I spit a caustic sputter-laugh at Ace. "Don't believe me?"

"Don't believe a Black Female who says she's concerned about me; bad habit, but what's a nigga ta do?" My meat-eyes drifted towards Melodie as cruel inhumanity blackened my Thoughts.

"Blatantly racist."

"Blame me mother, chummer. And while you're at it, explain something to me."

"Shoot."

"Melodie: here for two days of kinky Good-Bye Sex... offered freely to someone she won't be seen with in Public. Aside from being nearly incapable of Anger, what keeps me from flippin' out and kicking her to the curb? She **is** here for Standard Necropolis Local Excuses; I'll be one of many Sexual adventures she won't admit to having..." Melodie's Thought reached joyous heights; it took serious effort to keep my gaze from falling onto her. She saw my hand flexing, a sure sign that I was losing control to pleasure; I severed the neural connection to my Right Hand, saving her from Reality crushing her momentary illusion.

"Doesn't enter your brain that she *might* actually care for you... may feel something like **LOVE...**" My smile wasn't pure evil as I watched her jaw muscles move; evil actually cares about ***something***. I Saw her mentally prepare for my seed's flavor on her tongue and choke down a Joker's mad laughter at the Thoughts crashing/exploding in my skull.

"I'm not High enough to let that bullshit cross my Mind, Ace." I found myself briefly entertaining Thoughts of her attempts to Fuck a Nigga Senseless in hopes he'll stay by her side, but even then... Something I cannot describe yanks me back from the edge of Chaos and madness; I fell silent utterly fascinated by how... ***emotionless*** I Felt inside.

"Pointless." I exhaled/sighed the single word; Dead finality thumped as Ace breathed quietly.

"Now you see Why I'm just standing here, looking at my actions like a child watching some gruesomely fascinating show on TV..."

"Full of Questions you probably shouldn't ask, for your own mental stability; trouble is... you don't **care** about the Answers, do you."

"No... I don't." Truth rang clear within the following silence, bouncing around the emptiness.

"Most people throw a bash before they bail someplace heinous; that or they scurry out quietly. Bangin' this chica may well leave another Broken Heart in your wake... and you're trying to figure out Why this doesn't bother you." Ace turned his head slightly, the Ace of Spades covering his left eye solid blue/black/purple. "Almost as if there ain't shit **HUMAN** within ya."

My glance lingered; my answer came slowly.

"Jeanie's death, the shit-for-fuck Restaurants that came damn close to killing my passion for Cooking, and the constant abandonment by so-called Friends... not to mention my growing Council responsibilities; I'm stretched thin. Came close to returning to Nothing,

and the bullshit with my mother did ***NOT*** help matters. I Need a breather, Ace; Necropolis and its stagnant waters make that fuck-nigh impossible."

"That doesn't explain this; why not just leave the city? Ember did, though Ascendance made it impossible to ***remain*** among the Mortals. **YOU** are mere moments away from *possibly* doing more Emotional damage to someone who claims to care about you, and you're struggling to **UNDERSTAND *WHY...***"

"Why the inevitable outcome doesn't bother me at all; that about sums it up."

"So... you're **going** to play with her Emotions then."

"Not sure...; if it happens, fine."

"You don't care?" I shook my head slightly.

"Where does Seduction leave Physical Pleasure and stray into *Please Stay*?"

"Do you care?"

"I Need the Data, so maybe the answer is Yes; just don't Quote me on that." Behind us the Beast Within inhaled deeply.

"It slept through the act."

"Surprising; don't tell me it doesn't care." If I bothered to ask...

"She needs something Emotional from me; the Beast has no real Emotions."

"Rage..." I shook my head.

"Are **YOU** Ascending, Quick?"

"Hardly; Feels like I'm headed in the ***opposite*** direction."

* * * *

Appropriate.

Melodie's laugh suddenly stopped; her eyes darted about, searching for me in the crowded restaurant briefly before gazing through one of the windows lining the wall, scanning the neon soaked night outside, peering into the deepest shadows. I Manifested briefly, somewhat surprised when she spotted my black shape in the equally black dark shadow.

Are you OK? I smiled sadly; it didn't matter that she couldn't possibly see me, she somehow **knew** I suffered and ached. It is my Curse that those I care about know my Pain without hearing a single Word or catching the faintest glimpse of anguish on my features. I shook my head, forcing a smile I knew she couldn't see grace my lips; I've done enough Damage to Melodie. Even so, I Sent her warm Feelings and what, for me, passed as a pleasant Smile, severing the mental Connection before her Mind... or Soul... could return a signal or reject my effort.

I had things to do and Time, as always, was not an Ally.

* * * *

* * * *

From the Hidden Journal

The **only** Way to leave zero Physical Trace is Shadow Walking; this comes in handy for many different things, including Cheating: wanna pop in on your Lover, get a quickie, leaving only semen, sweat and memories? Pop into the Thoughtscape for a Shadow Jaunt; you can even remove **all** DNA evidence if you're really good, right down to the sweat you dripped on your lover's bed sheets. Shadow Walking is perfect for all clandestine actions and the Council makes use of it when preserving the Grand Illusion.

Angie is aware of Psions because her thirteen year old daughter Emerged... ***in CHURCH of all places!!*** Her child is Telekinetic; I was drifting through Random Thoughts when I caught the Scent from highly Focused thoughts: tell-tale Emergence-in-progress. Angie is an old High School Classmate, and something of an up-and-coming Social and **maybe** Political figure in Necropolis, **as well as the African American Community!!!**

She is also a Single Mother, a fan of my Tales, and **was** entertaining Thoughts of Making the First Move on ***me!!!*** Single Black Male... no diseases... *no Baby Mama Drama* and highly intelligent; I guess I pass for Prime Catch within her circles, minus my less-than-zero *official* cred flow. But I'm working on that and doing it in a manner which has more respectability than slangin' on Da Corner: professional cook and aspiring self-published Author. So... **NATURALLY...** Shit Happened.

And I became their Guide and Instructor into the World within their Reality; but first there was the matter of dealing with the witnesses to her Daughter's Emergence. I Shadow Walked a Cleanup Crew into the building, erased their memory of the event while Purging their bodies of residual Psionic energy and fixed any overt destruction; after that I contacted Section 8 and let them deal with those whose Minds and bodies are too far gone, or who cannot Forget and are plagued by terrifying recurring nightmares, dreams and/or hallucinations.

Normal Society is not ready to accept Psions as part of their Reality, so the Council perpetuates the Grand Illusion: Everything's Normal here.

* * * *

"So... **prayer...**"

"Is her Issue; think of it as brakes on a runaway car. Given time and training she may come to use her Gift without this *limiting* her ability, but there's a **big** catch: the kind of training that allows this will most likely reinforce her issue. That is: the harder she Prays, the more power she'll display. And I won't even go into **belief** here..." Angie laughed, waving away the Words with a more relaxed smile.

I understood why Angie didn't freak out and wished there were others with her intelligence and level-headedness; many Adult Minds simply shut down, refusing to accept the Reality before them. Being raised in the Church helped the tall, dark-skinned mother accept things; she almost found the Source of her daughter's Gift a God-given blessing. However, I explained the hard truth behind her daughter's Gift; linked directly to Praying, she couldn't use her Gift if she *wasn't* praying and risked using it ***every time she prayed*** unless she learned to control it.

"And... this Shadow Walking thing..." **NOW** we get to the part she wanted to talk about in earnest; so far I'd explained Shadow Walking as a form of teleportation, and I'd hope Angie would not press the issue. Many with religious upbringing chaff at the term **Shadow** Walking; when I told them that a common entry/exit requires a physical shadow their Thoughts immediately picture some hellish scene from a horror movie, complete with hell-spawn.

"Yes?"

"Can she do it?"

"Right now: no; only someone Skilled can Transport her without risk, and because she is My Charge, no one **can** unless they want a *really* nasty surprise: I Protect My Pack with ***savage*** Fury."

Especially considering the shit I **wasn't** telling her, like how her daughter's Issue seemed to attract some very Dark Thoughts, and at least one Foul Spirit. I didn't go into belief for one Reason; most

Christians believe in Satan, although in a decidedly back-handed manner. Still... Belief is **POWERFUL**; ***and opposites attract.***

* * * *

* * * *

Before her daughter's Emergence Angie knew certain things about the Power of Prayer; afterwards she spent many hours praying with her daughter, always afraid that somehow *something* would find Keisha's Gift offensive and come after her only child. When Silas Quick offered to train her beloved daughter she agreed, though she was wary of one thing. Silas wanted to wean Keisha from praying in order to wield her gift; his arguments were convincing, and now proved that she was correct: he understated things drastically.

LORD PROTECT US!!! Angie's car came to an immediate stop, the force actually activating the driver-side and passenger side air bags; yet **she** wasn't flung forward, merely winded. The brilliant beyond-white light she witnessed, along with a Sensation far exceeding what she **thought** was God's Presence, chilled her; it seemed to be everywhere, filling her with Peace, Comfort... and much to her amazement... **Fear**. Just before her daughter's prayer-fueled telekinetic outburst she saw... something.

* * * *

Richard squeezed his eyes shut and prayed with everything his young Mind could muster; he repeated

The Lord's Prayer fervently until only two Words thundered in his mind: **God PLEASE!!!!**

* * * *

"You call my daughter's Issue Prayer; do you have issues with God, Silas?" I could answer her question, but our conversation wasn't about my relationship with God. The question **did** present a rare opportunity and I seized it.

"**MY** Issue is as Simple as it is Complicated. My Gift is My Curse and comes from God Himself: All-Seeing... All Knowing... All Powerful... All Wise... and ***infinitely*** Unknowable."

"So?"

"My God isn't Limited by what we lowly Humans consider *Good...*" I shrugged; words will not Explain this. Ever. So... I smiled softly.

"I still don't get it; God..."

"**YOUR** God: God-the-Limited-to-What-I-Believe-is-Right." She inhaled deeply at my supposed insult; she screwed on Religious Debate Face, and I smiled. **It does an admirable job at pushing *down* Lustful urges**; I nodded, allowing my face to peer out just a bit more from my Dark-empowered hoodie. "My God is not limited to **only** doing what we Humans consider Good; for example... you get aroused when having an intelligent Conversation with a guy, especially a Black Male."

"What... profiling me... or..."

"**Both...** and it's pure instinct; another Issue: my first inclination is to Speak the Truth. So... I will give you something to Think about *before* you Think another Thought about seducing me... several actually. I Resonate with Souls that Need Honesty and Honor from their **LOVERS**; this means: if you find me at **all** sexually attractive, my God-given Gift... my Empathic Ability, will reinforce those

Thoughts within you. Ever wonder why you can't get some people out of your Thoughts? Now you can add this to the list of, 'He wore this cologne...' or 'They were dressed to kill...': *because of some screwed-up genetic ability* ***GOD*** *placed within the Human Genome... that's why.*" I could see her winding up for a rebuttal and decided to go for a kill-shot.

"You are curious about the Lifestyle... or to be precise: how I got involved; though you have no Thought to entering, much less *staying*, you are Intelligent and Wise enough to watch for Signs that I'm leaning that way... even though you have no clue *which* way is **that** way. Put simply, if we did Bump Uglies you'd be distracted by Thoughts of me-the-Dom, wondering if I'm trying to lead you into some Kinky Scene. Now... people often say that they can't think straight during sex; imagine *literally* being incapable of coherent Thought, and **not** because of Good Sex. I know it's rude, but Love won't have a damned thing to do with it; you can't think because my **God-**given gift *literally* clouds your mind. And while all of this may not make sense to you... *to me it means I can never be sure how much is my Gift,* ***and how much is because my chosen Partner is a willing participant***; again... all because of my GOD-given Gift. And if I curtail my Gift then I come off as cold and emotionless; yet this emotional detachment is the only way I can prevent someone from falling under the influence of my God-given Gift. **And** there's this: it is easy to Think about someone's Name or Image; consider this **carefully...**" She chuckles.

"You mean: don't Summon you if I slapped someone else on the butt, right?"

"Or the Random Thought about *I'd-Rather-be-Tied-to-whatever-than-be-HERE-with-YOU!!!* And I'm sorry to check your Laugh-Track again, but since you brought it up I have a very important Warning: You used the Term ***Summon...***; smacks of Spells, something the African-American Community has... ***issues*** with. The Church doesn't like the Old Ways and can't stand that some members hold true to those backwoods ways."

"Granma always said: *Watch what you Say, and Who you Talk About...*"

"'lest ya Summon up Ol' Man Scratch 'imself: that's how it goes back in the Big Easy." Angie stared at me; her smile eventually vanished when she realized **I was DEAD serious.**

"So... if my daughter were to pray to Satan..." I nodded grimly.

"You know I'm paranoid; what do you think it would take for me to Hear you Think my Name and instantly connect to your mind, hmmm? Do I have the right to enter your mind? No; but just thinking my Name when I'm in one of my more paranoid moods will connect our Minds if I'm not excessively careful... and you are but **one** Woman in my four decades on this Earth. All because of my God-given Gift; now you know why I told you about your daughter's Issue. You've often heard Preachers and Pastors speak about the Power of Prayer; you know your Bible, so you know *thou shall not take the Lord thy God's Name in Vain.* Even something like saying, 'God's gonna take this job from you...' will power her gift; the same thing goes for other *accidental* Prayers. From God *Damn* to calling His name during sex." Angie's mouth hit the floor and her eyes exploded as disbelief finally seized her Thoughts.

"And now for the **real** terror; remember those Preachers? They also like to say that Satan doesn't like it when someone prays; I don't know if that's true or not, but I **do** know that opposites attract. Those with their Gift inexorably bound to God-issue... or *any* religion-based issue, will draw the attention of some very nasty entities; breaking them of the issue won't prevent those things from popping up, but it keeps them from showing up ***every time you use your Gift***. If I may be so rude: I don't know of **any** Good Mother who wants their child exposed to danger, much less true and evil Hell Spawn."

"My mother would slap my mouth if I took the Lord's Name in vain; from what you're telling me..." Angie shivered. I let the truth chill her; indeed... even something as gracious as thanking God because you haven't seen someone in forever can, if left unchecked, activate her daughter's telekinetic gift.

"I will teach her how to use and control her Gift; your job as a mother is more difficult. Where you once hoped your child would be raised to Love God..."

"If I don't then she can cause a great deal of harm to someone else; I can't even take comfort that God has granted her this Gift... can I."

* * * *

"MAMA!!!"

Angie did not have time to acknowledge her dazed state; a deafening roar reached her ears and the rawest, most demonic-inspired FEAR gripped her. So powerful was this sensation that in less than a heartbeat it was the **only** sensation she knew, blowing away the peaceful bliss and dimming the white light within the car's interior; and so, the church raised African American single mother did what she'd been raised to do: Angie Prayed with her Soul, yielding to God's Will.

* * * *

The klaxon died the instant I brought up the screen; Data scrolled furiously as I watch the energy mass appear in front of a car. More mini-screens appeared as the car slammed into a Kinetic Field. Part science lesson and part horror story, the event I witnessed stretched even my imagination, and I **LOVE** Sci-Fi/Horror movies. Which explains a few things actually, like how I thought the car coming to a halt looked nothing like physics dictates; the back end didn't rise when the front slammed into an invisible wall of Force.

Confirmation: Energy signature - Fear.

Bad guys use surprise and other methods to make people afraid; the humanoid energy form was **created** from Fear... or fearful Thoughts and Emotions. Because I was viewing it through several bio-tech filters it has only shape; I wasn't in the Fear downpour the car's passengers had to experience.

Confirm: Amplifier Signature detected; Resonant outburst imminent. That didn't sound good. As the Denizen approached the car a brilliant white/blue light pulsated from the passenger's side; a smaller screen opened near the upper left corner of the main screen with data rapidly scrolling down it as all sorts of calculations were made, checked and verified.

Security of Echo One?

Nominal; no breech detected.

So where's that thing going? Command Central didn't answer; it was busy alerting me to what I was seeing. The invisible glow from the headlights suddenly became white/blue and locked on to the Denizen's body. The thing flew backwards, as if dragged from behind by its middle, but what I was watching was the Power output. There was definitely a Telekinetic in the passenger's seat, but the Output was *clearly* from two separate people, only **one** of which was within the vehicle. The other signal, while powerful, was not Focused or Controlled. The Denizen struggled against the beam briefly; the energy lost is blue tint, becoming intense white.

Source of the Amplification?

Source located; Emergence in progress.

* * * *

From the Blackened Scroll:

I am an Empath. I do not Read Minds, I Know the Soul; Thoughts and Emotions and their interaction with the Mind (conscious and sub-conscious) are easily Seen and Known, sometimes without actually *LOOKING* for them. Like all Emergences I went through a traumatic experience; in my case it was dying. As a child I had spinal meningitis; I can clearly recall the Night I emerged, my Empathic talent kicking in full force. I was in the hospital and feeling very sleepy; so I nodded off, and began a Journey I will never forget. I was at peace, a Peace so total, so filled with warmth and LOVE that it makes me smile even now. Up ahead there was a soft white light; it Felt Pure... Good and Wholesome. That's where I wanted to be and pulled myself up to run towards it; as I stood up I Noticed figures standing beside my path, lining the sides and going on and on. I think they extended into that soft white light, but one of the figures pulled away from the side.

He wore a black fedora and long black coat; I thought it was my grandfather. He was still alive however; didn't matter to me then - I Knew what he Felt like to me and **that** was my Grandfather. Only later would I learn his true identity: **Papa Ghede**. I remember looking around him and *thinking* about why he stood in my way; he didn't answer with Words, just Words-made-Feelings/Emotions. I Felt warm Concern and bright, joyous Amusement... and the cold black/blue which said, "That's not for you... not now." I remember Feeling Sadness douse me like a cold shower as he draped one arm over my shoulder, and wondering why I seemed taller and older. I turned around, those Thoughts obliterated by the swirling Chaos-blend of colors and sounds; his laughter deepened as I tried to slow their movement down, eager to see/See and know/Know what my Five

Senses were telling me. "In due time, son; come..." Next thing I knew I was back in the hospital, my mother seated to my left and looking worried.

"I wanna go back to sleep; that was good!" She exploded, telling me that if I went to sleep I would die.

I didn't care; if that sweet Peace was Death I *definitely* wanted to go back. There I wasn't constantly terrified that she'd follow through on her threat to **beat** me to death and simply make another child just like me only better. There I was **LOVED...** and when you're a kind secretly terrified by your own mother, who's just experienced the most peaceful Touch possible...

That is How I gained access to my Empathic Power; from that moment on it became impossible to Lie to me. I'd Hear the Lie echo within your words; if I concentrated I could even See where the Truth was concealed. It appeared as an amorphous black glob surrounded by sickly yellow, and quite often that sickly yellow seemed to *surround* me; hindsight and experiences allow me Knowledge of what I did as a child: I'd entered the speaker's Mind. I used my Gift to survive, prying into people's Minds, laying their Souls bare before my Empathic senses with terrifying ease and utter disregard for their emotional security or personal Privacy. My Gift sharpened my Street Sense immeasurably, leading more than one to comment that I had a good head on my shoulders or seemed highly intuitive; it also Opened my Sight to Spirits and other manifestations unseen by the Human eye.

Like most kids I wondered if Heaven was Real; after my Emergence I **knew** Heaven was real. I also knew something else: if Heaven and Angels were Real, then so were Demons, Ghosts and every other entity, and perhaps those Places Grand Mothers used to scare children into behaving... **like HELL**. I also knew that most Humans could not See these things even **if** they believed in them; suddenly Magic made more sense. I wondered why it didn't die out when mathematics and science took over everything; at first I figured it was the same Reason religion didn't die out once science started explaining things: Faith has nothing to do with Science. Only something happened: Ghost Busters; Hollywood cooked up a pseudo-scientific way to capture and contain Spirits, and I put two-and-two together.

See... if you read or listened to certain stories, you discovered that some spirits were contained **within** objects... **Physical, *here-and-now*** things; over and over again I came across this concept, eventually figuring out that Magic was just another form of Energy. I also figured out just how dangerous **that** concept was; if *Magic* were a form of energy which Mankind could learn to manipulate, what stopped Mankind from capturing this energy or something like it and trying to manipulate its way into Heaven, circumventing Jesus, the Angels... ***even GOD?!?!*** I remember sitting outside when I had this Thought... and hearing that same soft chuckle from Papa Ghede. *Some things Mankind wasn't meant to Know... because he didn't fully Understand.* This is how I came to understand the lesson of Adam, Eve, **and the Tree of Knowledge** that more than one Pastor and Deacon attempted to drill into my young, ravenous Mind; my Gift grants me certain **Knowledge**, but that is not always a Good Thing.

THE WEIGHT OF HUMANITY

Finding Marcus was easy... too easy. The Sensations I Felt along my path were too familiar, and much more heartless than I remembered. Unfortunately I had other matters to deal with; I should have appeared in the Thoughtscape near Marcus' location, but there was turbulence as I made my way there. Turbulence is rare; when I've encountered it in the past, someone was *trying* to prevent travel through a specific area of the Thoughtscape. I Felt something shift the turbulence, recognizing the intelligence behind the action by instinct alone; I threw up my left arm just in time to block the searing, dark-purple/puke-neon-green energy blast. It splashed over my arm guard, twisting itself into thick, rotten-flesh colored vines with thorns: Psionic Spell energy... and very powerful; razor sharp blades leapt from my armguard as I rolled over, Traveler in my right hand. I swept the short blade across the remaining dead-vine husk as I willed myself into Reality. I didn't stay there long; before I hit the ground I was back within the

Thoughtscape... close to the spot where I'd first felt the turbulence.

You're good. I didn't reply. Whoever attacked me was outside of the immediate physical area; anyone within the Turbulence would show up as oddly formed Sounds as the twisted-wind-like energy either left their form or moved around it. ***The strong, silent type; just like your Friend.***

If they could See me, they were smart enough to not crack jokes about my appearance; to most things within the Thoughtscape I look like ninja wearing a ceramic mask etched with one line slicing diagonally from left to right and two others at the lower end that formed an arrow. On either side of the arrow's shaft there were two smaller lines and all of the lines were steel-gray black. Whoever my attacker was, they were *very* careful about the Words they Spoke as well; Words come from Thoughts and are especially easy to Track if fueled by emotion. "The Thought Speech may **SOUND** feminine, but there is no gender guarantee." Remembering Lord Quick's warning during my early training I moved slowly towards the house; I Listened for any other change in the Turbulence while planning my next move. Nothing disturbed the Turbulence and **that** was interesting; if they were stalling for time...

Bitter cold choked my lungs; I'd been Forced into Reality!!! That takes serious Power; only time it's ever happened before was during training with Silas... and dealing with three very twisted old hags my second week in college. I barely managed to survive their attack. However, I was running solo then and made a Rookie Mistake; this time I did something different. Instead of jumping back into the Thoughtscape I quickly stuck Traveler into the ground, extending my forefinger and index the instant the black blade stopped. Overhead the clouds flickered/flashed; without warning a huge lightning bolt tore through the snowy night, but it didn't slam into me as I'd planned. Not that I minded, since I wasn't sure it **would** find me; I **was** sure of one thing: if my foe or foes had those things within them, lightning is something they **do not** want near them. Electricity crackled and hissed, *spreading over the house and ground in the shape of a webbed, egg-shaped dome!!* I extended my Senses into the Thoughtscape; the turbulence wasn't there.

MARCUS!!!

* * * *

Daphne looked like such a slut, bobbing her head on my cock; I **should've** enjoyed her experienced ministration, but I couldn't. I **COULDN'T**; it was as if I was looking down at myself being blown by some slut/cunt/whore MILF eager for Strange Dick, even if that Dick is attached to the guy her daughter's madly in love with. The longer I observed the scene the less I cared; flashes of Memory illuminated everything, and I saw Helen's face... her body covered by a white gown. I

should've Felt something; there **should've** been some Emotion... even Rage would've been welcome. Nothing. Not even the cold which dominated my Soul when... when Helen begged me to go too far; I had a choice then. I have a choice now; one Thought and Daphne would be dead a thousand different ways. One Thought and I could do whatever I wanted, sure that her mind would ***never*** be able to dredge up one Memory; one Thought and one Human Life would be forever destroyed. And yet... with these and more swirling through my Mind, **there was NO EMOTION BEHIND THEM**.

Daphne worked hard; she was Thinking about how my sperm would feel sliding down her throat. Apparently she enjoys swallowing, as the Thoughts inflamed the already raging Lust-inferno coiled around her brain and spine. Yet I found myself staring at my **own** Thoughts: *Reach down and tear her skull open; fling her brains over the walls and end her immoral ways.* Yes... I could do these things... ***easily***; I just didn't **care** to do them. It would take Anger, and I cannot Feel ***any*** emotion. Daphne even deep throated my member; she pulled free when I didn't respond... and again: **I Didn't Care!!!**

MARCUS!!!

My name; I Heard it. I *should've* felt something; there *should've been* ***some emotion*** *attached to it.* Nothing. I Sensed Thoughts and though I didn't Feel any Emotion, there **was** a Sense of Trust within the other Mind. I Sensed instructions within the mind, the

Thoughts requested reminding me of the Nightmare Time: when beautiful, trusting Helen still breathed, and there was **no** emotion attached to my actions as I Overdose Daphne. I compressed the Sensation of an orgasm and the biological impulses that came with it and forced her Mind to experience them simultaneously; an instant later I shut her Mind down, sending her into a deep REM sleep. I stared at her as she shuddered beneath the mental onslaught, crumbling to the floor in a spasmodic heap.

Only then did I Notice the form hunched over a sword; the blade glowed black, and I watched it pulsate: an ethereal heartbeat-rhythm I Knew. Penance; his name is Penance and he is my Brother. Those Thoughts came from him; I was puzzled at first, but then I Heard an angry snarl, and its Anger was directed at my Brother. I Heard the Chains before I formed the Thought; a small shadow soared into the air, moving from my left to my right. If it thought itself safe, impalement on my Chain ended the notion brutally and swiftly. A Sound... a Real Sound... touched my physical ears; I processed it slowly: Carrie. She was the Source of the physical sound.

* * * *

The shield evaporated; pressure I hadn't Noticed suddenly fell away and I willed myself into the Thoughtscape. To my right and slightly behind me someone howled in brutal agony; I didn't turn to find out who or why because of the **very** powerful Anger undercurrent rolling just over the physical ground. It appeared as if there were multiple attackers after all, and they were not prepared to deal with **two** skilled opponents working together. The only problem with that: Marcus wasn't Focused on combat. My Blood-Brother's Thoughts were elsewhere despite the Chain keeping one attacker restrained; and while it may seem obvious *where* his Thoughts were, that's true ***only*** if you have zero clue about his Past. I didn't know who the Female was, but I knew **what** she was doing; the worst part of this: Marcus wasn't *within* his physical body. He had control over what it did but it's a stretch to say he **felt** anything; the nerves sent the signals to the brain and the brain cells received the input, but his Conscious and Sub-conscious Mind got nothing. I knew how bad his Detachment was when I Saw him Shadow Walk into Thoughtscape; Marcus wore the dull black armor of a Hound, with modifications he'd made himself: My Brother wore the Armor of a Frozen Soul.

Chains; there's someone else.

They are retreating; it is good to see you again, Brother.

Likewise, though I wish it were under better circumstances. You look a bit stiff. He shrugged slightly, turning his head slowly towards the captured Essence.

Perhaps this one can help explain why this was necessary.

I'll take care of that; you see to your girlfriend, Brother. I heard her cry out.

So did I; I would like to speak with our attacker later. Meaning he fully expected me to leave the scumball alive long enough for his merciless ministrations; as Hounds, Marcus and I were known for truly heinous, often vile interrogation techniques. I appeared next to the bleeding body and gazed into dying blue-gray eyes.

Make it fast, Brother; this one won't last long.

* * * *

Comfort. Penance's presence gave me Comfort. As I passed through the ceiling I encountered a Spirit; it gazed at me with dead eyes watching me as I passed by. I ignored it; it hadn't attacked me and when it **had** the chance to Possess my physical body it remained where it was, so I allowed it to continue to Exist for the Moment. I pondered asking it why it refrained, and if it was still there when I passed that way again I would make it tell me why it stayed away from an Empty Shell. When I arrived at Carrie's body I expected to see a corpse; she sat upright in her bed, breathing heavily and staring into the snow-glow darkness. Fear dominated her Thoughts, and the Stain seemed drunk with Fear's energy; I found this... strangely fascinating. Tearing it out of Carrie's Mind would cause irreparable damage; if she were to live any attempt must be done carefully.

Or...; without warning I wrapped a Chain around my girlfriend's neck, strangling her. She grabbed at nothing, clawing at the sensation in vain; I squeezed tighter and watched as the thing became highly agitated.

Leave her and do no harm. The thing uncoiled from her Mind rapidly, yet it remained within her Thought patterns, concealing itself with the horrendous Terror filling her Essence, contorting it into a bloated and oozing mess. I felt my right eyebrow rise slightly; L.J. once taught me how to turn Pleasure's sensation into agonizing pain, and I decided to try this technique on the entity, forcing Carrie to experience **PLEASURE** instead of Terror. It didn't work completely, but it cut the Stain's drug supply judging from its reaction.

You did not obey; your choice then. I opened my hands slowly, concentrating on how electrons move and create electricity; I relaxed my Chain's grip around her neck... only to slap my hands against her temple, pouring electrical current into her brain. The Method is crude, and most likely overkill; I stopped once the thing, screeching like a wounded banshee, fled into the Thoughtscape. I Tracked it easily, though there is a distraction I found... disturbing... maybe. I could easily have killed Carrie and I didn't care... ***but I Feel like I WANT to care.***

Tag, Penance; tend to Carrie's wounds while I see what our prisoner has to say. I was still staring at her barely breathing body when Penance appeared on my right hand side. **THAT** made me smile slightly.

* * * *

* * * *

Dominique?

Yes? She sounded pissed, not that I blame her. I **was** contacting her simply because I needed her skill.

Marcus' girlfriend's got some serious damage; he really did a number on her when he extracted that thing from her.

It's an infestation. There are accounts coming in from nearly every Hound...

Since when did you...; never mind. Can you help her? I've gotta see to Marcus.

And WE will talk when you return, Biz be damned, Penance.

* * * *

He's still alive.

Stasis crystal; Penance... we have a serious problem on our hands.

What did you get from him? Your girlfriend will be fine by the way; I asked...

Dominique; I Felt her Mind. She's grown powerful. As for the trouble I mentioned: I do not believe that thing comes from Earth.

So... alien invasion attempt? Sounds a bit far fetched; from what I've read in the Black Journal, alien Minds don't Think like ours.

In theory they don't; in practice we may be surprised how alike our Minds are. We feel certain things like Love, Hate, Anger and Joy; there is every reason to believe an alien race has similar concepts.

Concepts like... infection. An empty frozen Feeling gripped my gut. *Let's suppose you're right; it* ***would*** *explain why Section 8 is involved. They've been experimenting with creating Artifacts for decades.*

They have access to Psion lore and perhaps a few test subjects; nothing stops them from experimenting with a few human-alien hybrid items, especially considering they have access to no less than three different alien species.

How do you know this?

He volunteered the information. I didn't check; Marcus definitely Mind Raped the dying Agent judging from the empty gaze permeating his eyes.

He doesn't know who the mastermind of this nightmare is by any chance...

If he does it may trigger the Thought Bomb I Sensed; its creation is crude, but *VERY* ***effective. I suggest we return to the Grounds and share information.***

I'll try to contact Quick...

No... just the three of us.

Any reason you wanna leave Lord Quick and the others out of this?

Nothing I can state with any certainty; it is... a Feeling based on what I've seen so far.

And that is?

There were no attacks directed at Lord Quick, and the attacks against us were traps; they wanted us... *alive.*

And there was something else; the traps were devoid of overt Psion involvement. That would give Silas Reason **and** Excuse, and I didn't think there was any Free Talent willing to piss him off, especially since he'd definitely call on Meanstreak, Ace and more than a few Council Resources.

We still need a Cleanup Crew here... unless you've got an idea.

None comes to mind.

Hurry Home gentlemen; I'll see to Cleanup while you Shadow Walk.

Marcus smiled slightly; I frowned. I hadn't sensed Dominique's presence and was sure Marcus didn't Call to her.

"Let's go, and stay close Marcus." The plan hadn't fully formed in my mind, and I wasn't about to let it get there... especially since I wasn't sure Dominique wasn't Listening. We entered the Thoughtscape quickly, but I wasn't heading towards Darkhaven Manor just yet.

"You're planning a detour?"

I took one deep breath, held it for one heartbeat, and exhaled; I Felt Power gather at my feet, swirling and churning invisibly until waves splashed against my calves. When the waves reached my hands I was Focused and ready; I performed the *kuji-in* swiftly, molding the energy with my Thoughts. I completed the summoning, ending with both hands open and fingers splayed, thumbs and index fingers touching to form a single flame.

A thin gray line stretched into existence before me; it spun rapidly, darkening in splotches until the funky looking cloak manifested completely.

"Suit up, Chains; we're going to visit the Council." And I had one stop to make before that.

* * * *

Blacksoul. I knew Marcus had Gone Under again, but the realization that this part of his personality had manifested and taken a NAME...

"Are you sure Dom?" I asked softly, my thoughts racing as everything crashed like massive white-capped waves over granite cliff.

"I am. Though I wonder... you're not here to ask about your Brother..." I sighed.

"Lord Quick discovered one of those things within Gina." I waited for my most recent ex-girlfriend to show some emotion; instead she took a deep, cleansing breath and exhaled slowly. If that was the extent of her anger then I was truly fortunate... or just too close to the situation to really grasp the hidden meaning; either way I knew I was no closer to settling things with Dom.

"I won't ask if you still care for her; I know you too well Snape." I cringed, snorting a soft chuckle at the use of my high school torment of a Nick Name. "Those you care for, you will always care for; Lord Quick chose correctly when he chose you."

"Glad you approve; I'm not so sure. All I ever wanted was..."

"Normal? Need I remind you of our adventures in the Thoughtscape? There are those who whisper the name Penance with terrible reverence even now."

"You've been back?" I was startled... and more than a bit worried; she'd become a powerful Warlock in one side reality we got stuck in, and it took everything I had to get her back. Of course, that's when I was nothing more than a skilled thief caught up in a madman's power grab.

"I maintain a connection to the High Council there... thanks in part to **your** efforts to save me."

"I..." Crap; stuck in the middle of *another* high stakes adventure and once again: flustered by someone I...

"Which reminds me: I came across something while reading The Blackened Scroll."

Sometimes a Warrior does not get the luxury to choosing the Battlefield, and must adapt quickly; this is known as Taking a Wide Stance.

"Dom..." She paused, gazing through my eyes; I knew I could keep her from Seeing my Thoughts if I chose, but this was not a time for deception.

"Don't, Lawrence; I know how you feel about me. I... I just wanted to know if you'd be here if I needed."

Just like that everything seemed to settle down inside my head... but more importantly: my Heart stopped wringing itself into knots. I wasn't **completely** at ease, but at least I knew why Silas said what he said: ***To protect the Future***. Mine. Dominique's. Marcus'... even the new kid Cypher; something was coming and it worried Silas enough that he took up the challenge to protect what he held dear. I just hope it wouldn't cost me as much as it cost the Old Man... and somehow... I wasn't sure my hope was going to be enough.

"I give my Word of Honor: I will always be at your side, Lady Dominique." She smiled softly; my heart skipped a beat and I accepted her silence as thanks. She closed her eyes briefly; when they opened I found myself staring into dark orbs with vibrant silver, blue and white sparkles dancing within their depths. I'd seen this before... when I told her I loved her; I meant those Words, and now... I knew... **KNEW...** she loved me. And for the first time in my life... I Felt **FEAR**.

"Now suit up Champion; you'll need the protection. I'll Send you what I read in the Blackened Scrolls as you prepare." I bowed before leaving her, stepping into the darkened room I kept within the back house on the Manor's grounds.

This is what old folks meant by Growing Up Fast. No chance to Think... barely enough time to react; and in the end... all you can do is hope you've done the right thing. Sighing heavily I forced myself to calm down; I was about to walk into the chambers where the Council of Psions conducted their business, and I wanted to be ready for anything. Sickening; can't even enjoy the comfort of the Woman I Love. Lord Quick... I never Understood...; now I wish I didn't.

THE COUNCIL

"You are silent."

"Thinking deep Thoughts." I heard Marcus sniff the not-air within the Thoughtscape. He looked awkward in his old Hound gear; the cargo pants seemed to shift contrary to his movements, as if they wanted to morph into something different yet were restrained somehow.

"You smell like White Lily." Dominique's perfume; I smiled and risked the brief moment, remembering her warm embrace before I left the Manor's grounds. I appeared before her, clad in the gear Lord Quick gave me on my eighteenth birthday; it was pure ego: I wanted her approval. And got the warmest, most sublime hug I'd ever received; I didn't conceal my Emotions as I remembered that Moment; I let it fill me as fresh air fills the lungs.

"Deep Thoughts... and precious few Happy Memories. We're on a fact-finding mission and I don't expect to find anything without serious effort... or dangerous accidents."

"You expect combat?"

"I don't know what to expect."

"Worse than combat then; I shall take precautions." As I Felt Marcus shift Psionic energy around him I split my attention between following the Path of Shadows and reviewing what Dom Sent into my Mind.

* * * *

From the Blackened Scroll:

Problems with Authority

The Council does not get involved in Mundane affairs.

For the most part this is True, though it **does** lead to some serious Conflicts of Interest. Take for example the case of a Child Molester; if no one involved possesses a Psionic talent the Council will not interfere. This causes no end of conflict as the majority of Council Members are Empaths; not only are they capable of Knowing a molester's intentions, they are perfectly capable of stopping him or her; between their own Gifts and the Hounds, the Council can hunt down any Mundane molester and stop their sickening rampage. They can even snitch the molester out to local authorities, and this is where the main Conflict Issue arises; in order to maintain this hands-off distance the Council must **Mind Rape** individuals. This is known as the ***Prime Conflict.***

The Charlatan wanted to control the Thoughts and Actions of **every** Human Mind; this strips Humanity of Free Will. Imagine for one moment: if you saw someone and the Thought occurs to you, "He's/she's cute/sexy/hot..." you'd be in violation of his Thought-Law and subject to virtually **immediate** punishment. Across the World there are examples of such Thought Law; in America, particularly the South, Blacks and Whites were ***legally*** forbidden to marry. Imagine if using an attractive model to sell your product earned you immediate Thought Reconstruction: having your Mind reprogrammed to prevent such Thoughts; this is what the Charlatan's rule would have been like. And you can **forget** the concept of religion entirely; Faith is a matter of Thought and Soul. The Charlatan saw religion as something **he** dictated, ***not*** a matter for individuals to ponder. You couldn't even Love and Fear God without his express permission, and **he** did not like Humanity loving or fearing anyone other than himself.

You are Told who to find attractive; you are Told who to marry. You do not have a say about how many children you may have. Forget Gender Equality; there would be no Basic Human Rights. You don't even have the luxury of deciding to visit an old friend, surprise your wife with a gift, or even hold your child; **every Thought... every Idea... is *given* to you by the Charlatan!!** The Council saw the madness within his supposed Utopian World; at first they tried to convince him of how foolish he was. After he killed three Council members they knew there would only be one way he'd ever stop.

Enter the General, and another grand Conflict. It is painfully easy to kill the physical form; it is infinitely more difficult to *kill* a Council Member. In order to ensure their complete destruction one must obliterate even their Thoughts. Leave enough Thought/Soul energy cohesive and they **will** regenerate; they may not take the **exact** same physical form, but their Soul and Thoughts **will** reform. It was the General who discovered just how this happened, and in doing so became the first Council member considered truly Ascended. While there is more than enough energy within **this** universe to reform, it is much easier to draw energy from a parallel universe, one where a version of you Exists. This Knowledge very nearly shattered the

General's mind, yet it also allowed him to disperse the Charlatan's Thought/Soul energy to a degree where he was no longer a threat. This is why the Council believed the **General** to be such a threat; he could, if he chose, live forever by siphoning the Thoughts from his parallel counterparts.

Yet the General's Ascension brought more than this; over time he came to Understand the nature of Ascension, and is instrumental in the present understanding of the Thoughtscape. He also stumbled across Knowledge he felt detrimental to Human development: Humanity's genetic development has been tampered with by extraterrestrial life forms.

* * * *

Shocking? Hardly; God **gave** Mary her first child, Jesus. Technically, that makes Jesus an Alien Life Form; while some Christians will argue against this, I stress this: **GOD** created the code. If anyone **can** create a Human it is God; arguing against Jesus being an alien means you do not believe God to be capable of creating a Human being perfectly capable of passing such rigorous Human inspections as *circumcision* and casual glance (five fingers and toes, two lips, two ears, one nose, etc.) In fact the Bible is *littered* with such examples; it would be much later that one of the Council discovered the General's discoveries and pieced together a disturbing truth: less powerful entities have **continually** tinkered with genetic manipulation. Across the known Multiverse this is a universal Truth; in our own universe we have specific examples. Just look at the Egyptian imagery of **their** Gods and the Monsters of Greek and Sumerian mythology; the Council knows these as proof of genetic experiments. It is **FACT**, and capable of shattering current Human Civilization irrevocably.

What makes this Knowledge troubling to the Council is this: not every alien race is benevolent. My battle with Jerry revealed this, and revealed a race capable of creating semi-sentient entities from Thoughts!!! Just imagine the horrific possibilities; pulling together the Thoughts of murderers, forging them into one cohesive Killer and unleashing it upon an unsuspecting society. Forget Jack the Ripper as a

Human being; Jack the Ripper - Denizen of Human Thought is beyond terrifying. You can't blow his head off and end his reign of terror; **he'd reform and continue killing!!** Now remember: **The Council does not involve itself in Mundane matters**; does this include an alien race drawing the worst Human Thoughts together and creating a somewhat Human monstrosity?

I've already had to Answer such Questions. Someone *turns* into a child molester and doctors discover a tumor in the brain that may well be the cause; imagine this tumor resulting from some alien race tinkering with re-wiring the Human brain. **However, the subject is not Psionic!!!** According to the Council, we do ***nothing!!!*** Never mind the Fact that a psionically talented alien race just screwed with a Human Mind, the Mind belonged to a Mundane; if that doesn't terrify you, how about the molester who successfully *adapts* to those heinous Thought-Implants and becomes a treasure trove of such Thoughts. Do we stop the alien race from mining the Mind for it, or, because the Mind belongs to a Mundane, do we sit by and do nothing?

Like the General, I possess Knowledge which can destroy Society. There's a ship on its way to our planet with one goal: take samples of the Human population. I don't know why they want this sample, but I do know how many it plans to take: **Thirty-three percent!!!** This is what the probe determined is an adequate sample; all I know is this: that's close enough to the one-third predicted in the **RAPTURE** to throw humanity into utter chaos!!

And knowing this I am faced with a serious crisis, not just as someone who Loves and Follows God, but as a Council Member. Collectively the Council has the power to **stop** this ship before it completes its mission; ***DO WE?*** I **KNOW** this is not the Rapture, for those taken won't be going to Heaven. All well and good to Know this, but trying to convince the **entire WORLD** is not nearly impossible, but there is no **proof** other than the Word of someone with an ability many don't think exists outside of demonic/magical power.

Not to mention how impossible **all** of this sounds; aliens tinkering with how Humans think... a ship headed our way tasked with snatching up a number equal to the Rapture, **coming at a time many consider the End of Days...** yeah: uphill battle for the Council, *and not all of them believe me about the ship!!!!* So the natural Question is: *what **DOES** the Council consider worthy of its involvement?*

* * * *

Petty shit, though it may not sound petty to some. The Council prevents Psions from enslaving Humanity. How can I call that petty? Easily considering some of the Experiences I've had; the Psionic parent forcing their Child to behave a certain way...

Yep; the Council doesn't interfere in Mundane matters but has **zero** problems fucking with the Family Unit **whenever there is something it considers an Abuse of Power.** I've hunted down people who turned their Gift against others, including all manner of sexual predators, serial killers and even managed to stop a would-be mass murderer; yet because I'm a Council Member I cannot *legally* touch any non-psion guilty of those same crimes. And this is the Council's Reasoning...

Free Will extends to the sanctity of Thought; Humanity must be allowed the freedom to Think without being subject to the Will of one individual. I actually understand the concept; I do **not** agree with its carte blanche application. I understand the concept based on something most know: the Thought *I'm gonna choke the life outta you!!!* It's perfectly Normal to **have** this Thought, just as it is socially unacceptable to turn it into Action... **under normal circumstances**; there are certain extremes where it is almost accepted, but they **ARE** extreme circumstances.

Then there's Punishment; society continues to grapple with the concept of Fair and/or Just Punishment for Crimes. The Council is no different, and it has access to punishment horrendous enough to chill the Souls of the Dead, Living **and** unborn. There is a term used by most high schools kids: **Brain-Fried**; I've cooked someone's gray matter inside their skulls, so I know that term as real-Life. If that's too gruesome, how about we do what the alien race does: re-wire the

Human Mind *physically*; trust me when I say: Mind Surgery is not easy. And what **is** the proper punishment for raping someone's **MIND?!?!?** Whatever it is, every Council member **must** endure it, as Mind Raping is a common practice, not to mention it happens to be the easiest way to Shadow Walk.

Yep: Shadow Walking is Mind Rape; you can call it a mild form if you like, but considering I've known more than one Woman who's endured the physical Hell I take a different view: **Rape is Rape - End-of-File.** Just because you use the Thought energy to enter the Thoughtscape doesn't mean you have ***permission*** to enter someone's Mind. Here's something: if the Thought leaks from the Mind, does that count as Mind Rape? The Council doesn't believe so, leaving a **huge** Loop Hole open. Some letch walking down the street thinking about and drooling over a pair of jiggling Double-D tits doesn't count despite pouring raw Sex-Thoughts into the air: that is considered fair game; the Female with that smirk on her face pouring Sex-Thoughts about a sexy guy (or gal) into the air: fair game.

But the teenage Mind Reader who pries into someone's mind for the answers to question three on his civics test, what to do about him or her? The Empath who Influences someone for sexual purposes is one thing; the Empath who shuts down a bully's Mind: is that something different? Then there's Remote Viewing, the most difficult Gift to police; what is the punishment for being a Psionic peeping Tom/Jane? Better... **when** is punishment administered in such cases? It may seem stupid to punish mom for peeping on her son, but does the Council have the *right* to stop her from Following him on his first Date... prom Night... hanging out with the guys... **those weekends with his father whom she despises?!?!?** What does the Council do about the ***kid*** with this Gift?

"Dad, I get these... dreams about Mom; it's like I can see her..." Mother and Father - Mundane; is this covered by the Hands Off rule? What if one parent knows the nature of their child's gift; does the Council have the right to prevent them from abusing their child's talent? *Check up on your Mom/Dad and keep me informed*; can you imagine the chaos? I don't have to Imagine; I've had to clean up the **aftermath** of *SEVERAL* such matters because the Council couldn't determine if they should get involved and one parent got **killed** in the ensuing nightmare.

* * * *

Now let me discuss the Government of the United States and the Council. We **do not** work *for* the Government; though barely two hundred years old the United States is perfectly placed to take advantage of those possessing Psionic Gifts. Consider the basic Gift of Remote Viewing; now we move from the kid peeping in on his sister taking a shower to the Spy capable of reading sensitive documents anywhere in the world from the comfort of the **toilet!!** An accurate Remote Viewer is every Intelligence Agency's wet dream, surpassed only by the operative capable of killing someone while leaving ***ZERO*** trails. How about turning someone close to the target into the Assassin's Bullet; perhaps the biggest question: **HOW DO YOU DEFEND AGAINST SUCH A WEAPON?** All of the lie detector tests and interrogation/torture sessions in the world won't reveal Psionic tampering, ***believe me!!!*** Or how about this for a nightmare scenario: **Shadow Walk a thermonuclear device into the White House**; the only things required are the nuke... and someone inside the white House who happens to be thinking a Thought. Joke all you want, but there are those within **every government in the Free World** who consider this a very real possibility. Why?

Because of genetics; eventually there will be a mass Emergence. All over the world Psions will display the vast array of Gifts capable. Remember that genetic tampering the Council discovered... the same one which Ancient Alien Theorists say is a **possibility?** Eventually someone got paid to consider it as Something Real, and they were contacted by the Council. Apparently this person was **Latent**; latent Psions possess the *potential* but have not fully emerged. In short, **they are not Mundane**, so the Hands Off Rule doesn't apply. From that moment on, the Council and the United States Government agreed to maintain the Status Quo; the Council would steer clear of **all** Mundane matters, including being banned from holding political office. Since no one could predict who would display Psionic talent or even ***when*** it would happen, **and** because the Council considers Latents as Psions, the G-Man blackmailed the Council into sharing responsibility for their development. As Payment, the Council Opened his Mind and filled it with part of its vast collective Knowledge, literally driving him insane.

That was the Council's first failure; they learned quickly, though in my opinion they **forgot** the lessons from History. Many leaders and nations consulted Wise Men, wizards and oracles; in some cases they were Psions, in others the Council found itself dealing with shards of the Charlatan's powerful intellect.

* * * *

The original Council believed Mankind/Humanity would grow to accept Psions; the current members are not certain this acceptance is a good thing. It has *potential*, but there are a few flaws in the Logic, flaws only recently revealed. One problem to arise: Nationalistic Pride; no one should think poorly of **anyone** who is proud of their Nation and heritage. However, one must understand the nature of Nations in general, especially this facet: **they are often forged through wars and other conflicts.**

Today people complain about Big Brother; just imagine if Big Brother not only existed, but was founded by one or more Psions. The Council does its best to avoid becoming Big Brother; which is what makes the G-Man's blackmail attempt so damned laughable. The **last** thing the Council wants is control over individual Minds to the point where it *gives* people Thoughts to think; we are currently busy doing things to secure **Humanity's continued survival** and have never had any interest in ruling the World: too much micro-management. As is stated by one of our members, "We are perfectly content in allowing Mundanes the opportunity to fucking shit up royally by believing themselves to be Masters of Everything." However, there will always be someone who **thinks** they have the answer; give them enough power and they will make the attempt. And these are **MUNDANES**, just your regular Joe or Jane; people are worried about the

Government or some Corporation prying into their life-extensions on the internet (more commonly called Social Media), yet a Tech Head has more access than the Government **and** isn't restrained by the Law. Forget Identity Theft; how about stealing every dime from everyone in the U.S. and dumping it into some terrorist's or Columbian/Mexican drug dealer's off-shore account. Don't like the opposition party? **KILL 'em ALL!!!** Force people to vote for your candidate with a simple Thought, or Force everyone to buy your product; though many consider this strictly something a Corporation would do, ***what if a drug dealer wanted the entire WORLD hooked on his shit?!?!? Impossible? NOT AT ALL*** if the dealer possesses enough empathic ability... **like the Charlatan**; these are the situations the Council deals with.

And make no mistake, there **are** some matters the Council *never* wants made public. During World War Two they were involved in keeping certain Psionic artifacts from falling into Hitler's hands; as to whether or not they could have prevented the Holocaust... ***The Council does not get involved in Mundane matters***. This includes the tragedy of 9-11: **Mundane Matter**; and in both examples, there were those who knew something horrible was going to happen. They were all Latents, so the Council could *assist* them; in the case of 9-11, Mundanes in Authority/Power Positions did not listen. Not only could the Council have **prevented** that tragedy, but the Hunt for bin Laden took ***HOW LONG?!?!*** With one Empath to hunt down his Mind and a Tech Head to control either a drone or cruise missile: job done in three days **MAX**; however... MUNDANE matter.

The Council cut its political teeth on some of the toughest situations ever recorded in history; along the way it's left a litany of mysterious figures: Sun Tzu for example, the Mad Monk Rasputin for another. One thing the Council is notorious for is altering the Memory of Mundanes involved with its business; this practice **continues** to cough up unexpected results, not to mention the different versions of events causing no end of nightmares for future historians.

* * * *

It is rare that a Mundane finds themselves before the powerful Council of Psions; I knew my Charges would need at least three such audiences before they felt confident enough to deal with their abilities and responsibilities, so I instructed them on protocol. Even so, I am proud of how long they waited before asking for their first audience; I am not, however, surprised that only L.J. approached the Council chambers. Marcus stood outside, joining the Ethereal Guards in a position of Honor. I know Meanstreak's pupil better than this; standing between the guards placed the invisible psi-chains he wore on his wrists at his sides, ready to assault the guards should the need arise. L.J. is just paranoid enough to plan for a violent escape, damn the supposed futility of facing thirteen Ascended Psions, each one a thousand times more powerful than he and Marcus combined.

"Welcome to the Council Chambers, young warrior; your Teacher speaks highly of you."

"I am honored to be here, Lady Victoria."

"You know of me?"

"Lord Quick has mentioned you often."

You are truly paranoid; did you think I would Seduce such a young pup?

You cannot help yourself; that is why I instructed him to wear Rainfall.

You have the most interesting Artifact collection, Lord Silas.

"How may we assist you, Face of Penance?" Only myself and Bogdan revealed our faces; the weathered countenance he wore today was not his preferred mask and I reminded myself to ask him later about his choice. If he expected to invoke Thoughts of the Mad Monk Rasputin within my former Student he failed miserably.

"During my training, Lord Quick spoke of the Mass Emergence; this event was, as I understand matters, a natural event. Recently I and my Friends have encountered something unnatural: presences within Mundane Minds that are... and are not... born of Human Psionic attempts."

"**YOU** did not teach him to be so polite, Lord Quick."

"Indeed; what's up, Penance?"

"We believe Section 8 is experimenting with the Lore the Council shares with them. The Infestations are not completely of this planet..."

"You mean... Alien." Bogdan's thick Russian accent aimed for contemptuous, falling far short if L.J.'s reaction is any indication.

"Correct, Lord Councilman; I regret not knowing your name..."

"I do not. Forgive my rudeness, but what makes you and your friends so certain these... *things*... come from outer space?"

"We have a prisoner..."

"**Ahhhhhh...**; you raped this prisoner's Mind for information then."

"On the contrary; we purged the Taint from their mind and during our attempt to patch him up his Thoughts leaked."

You HAVE taught him well, Quick!! I haven't heard such a smooth lie since my days in the KGB.

What are you looking for, Bogdan?

If Section 8 is **performing experiments on Psions, it isn't a stretch to think likewise about other Governments; I've heard rumblings in Russia about such experiments. Perhaps we should investigate more closely?**

"A compassionate act, one worthy of a Knight." L.J. bowed slightly.

"Do you believe Section 8 is attempting to force the Mass Emergence?" Harrison moved his forearms slowly, drawing L.J.'s notice; my former student didn't turn immediately, though the subtle twitch told me he wasn't comforted by Harrison's Voice or Tone. Then again... none of the Clan Cursed likes the Government Voice, and

Harrison is a true Master of United States Government-Speak.

"This is why I asked for an audience with the Council; my friends and I have come under attack from Section 8 operatives who possess this Taint. We ask the Council to investigate this matter."

"Begging pardon, Face of Penance: why do you and your friends not investigate this matter?" I was somewhat surprised to hear Da-Xia speak, and *completely* amazed when the beautiful Chinese woman pulled her hood from her head.

"Dealings with Section 8 are Council matters; my friends and I have more bland concerns at the moment."

"He avoids Thinking about something."

Prying into my former Student's Thoughts, Da-Xia? Rude.

"Necessary; he is trained by you, Lord Silas. Deception may be only a Tool to you, but it is one you use with the skill of a master surgeon."

"Very well," Lady Victoria said. "We will look into the matter and keep your former teacher informed."

"Thank you Lady Victoria; thank you, Council." L.J. bowed respectfully and took three steps backwards before turning his back on the Council; while his movements are standard protocol, I Noticed how he *forced* Respect into them.

* * * *

Marcus never moved when the opaque opal doors gave a muted groan; only when L.J. appeared on his left did the armored black man move, bowing to the Guard on his right before smoothly stepping after his best friend. He remained silent, following L.J. as they made their way down the alabaster hallway, although his Thoughts constantly probed the soft, warm glow radiating from somewhere overhead. Once they reached the grand foyer and its cool bluish marble floors and imposing columns crafted from stunningly somber, highly polished mist-gray stone, L.J. stopped and Marcus followed suit, yet neither spoke. Within seconds a small woman clad in gossamer blue robes floated across the floor towards them. Her eyes matched her robes perfectly, yet Marcus was more impressed by how the thin cloth concealed her feminine parts while revealing the tanned flesh of her arms, legs and trim, firm abdomen.

"We are honored by your presence, Face of Penance."

"It was an honor to be here, fair Alyssa. Please give my regards to your mistress and mother for me." Alyssa smiled and bowed her head, gesturing to the marble wall before them. No sound greeted their ears as a large wood door manifested from within the stone. L.J. bowed deeply, stepping purposefully towards the exit. Marcus followed silently and together they exited the impossibly large building. Marcus admired the infinite darkness just outside of the wide gallery; L.J. seemed to contemplate one of the massive columns for several seconds before tilting his head slightly, signaling his readiness. Marcus swung his head slowly, his eyes lagging behind the actual head movement; his armored legs flexed powerfully, and with a thought he was running full speed. As the armored Soul Hound entered the dark void, L.J.'s cloaked frame disintegrated; only when they entered the more comforting semi-dark of the Thoughtscape did Marcus speak.

"They expend a great deal of energy projecting immense scale, yet very little on grandeur. Somehow I expected... more."

"I don't know what I expected, but I've got what I needed from them."

"And that was...?"

"They know Section 8's infested with that thing and they know it isn't from Earth." Silence lingered between them as they ran through the chaotic expanse; Marcus spotted a familiar Thought below him and some distance to the left and frowned slightly.

"There's more; your silence says much."

"Yeah... I Felt one of them touch my Mind."

"You fought off the attempt?"

"Tried, but they weren't looking into my mind, just touching it, like a scared kid touching a frog or spider or something."

"Lord Quick's presence stopped them... or do you suspect something else..."

"Don't know and I don't care; what I **do** care about is the G-Man on the Council. He mentioned the Mass Emergence... asked **me** if I thought Section 8 was trying to force it."

"That **is** interesting, and poses more than a few questions about Section 8's interaction with the Council. Do you believe the G-Man has information he does not share with the Council?"

"Right now I wanna get back and talk to Dom; she knows something..."

"That is a conversation long overdue, Brother, though I feel your questions may cause more harm." L.J. did not reply; soon a large bamboo forest sprang into view.

"We'll find out soon enough bro; let's get back to the House."

AGAIN THE UNKNOWN

From the Blackened Scroll:

From its beginning the Council was flawed; considering its Human membership this is not surprising or unexpected. At first the members were more concerned with being and acting Wise when dealing with our kind: Psions. It wasn't long before something akin to a Military arm was seen as a necessary evil. This happened because of a long dead Free Talent: a Psion who isn't bound by Council dictates; known as the Charlatan he sought to control Humanity. He believed Psions were superior to Mundanes: humans without Psionic Gifts. When the Council finally decided to stop him the resulting Psi-War devastated Humanity and nearly wiped out the already thin Psionic gene pool.

And you don't get the whole *imprison the bad guy* spiel to this tale; the head of the military obliterated the Charlatan. In my opinion he did the right thing; because of his actions, however, the Council believed him to be the **next** Charlatan and banished him from the Council. They also prevented him from breeding, stating rather vehemently that they would kill any in his bloodline. Funny how that works: they were loath to kill the original Bad Guy but dead set on slaughtering the unborn to *prevent* what they perceived to be the next-in-line. Fortunately for the Council today, the past membership failed to carry out their threat.

As for the General, the Council has only themselves to blame; they chose him for several Reasons. First and foremost was his immense Empathic power. Military prowess was **third** in line; the second consideration was cunning. The Council recognized the Charlatan's threat beyond merely defeating his army, and sought out an Empath capable of out-thinking their adversary and any back-up plans he had in place. If it seems like I missed something, one must Understand How the Council Thinks; they sought someone with like-minded *tendencies*. The General accepted the Council's order to not bear offspring after much debate.

Enough to conceal his pre-emergence wanderings; after the War, he went back to wandering the World. The Council believed he was pondering his actions deeply and gave him space; in truth, he was watching the three women who'd born him children already. The Council would discover the Truth... on the day I obliterated Jerry; I am descended from one of the General's bloodlines.

* * * *

Necropolis is a cesspool despite its genteel Southern appearance; the power players like to think themselves above Big City problems. Pure lie of course; I *personally* know of enough skeletons to make a Big Easy cemetery shudder, and they all have one thing in common: **SEX**.

Autumn and Winter are the perfect Seasons to reveal the city's obsession with the Horizontal Tango, and its adherence to a grand Southern Genteel Tradition: **Human Activity STOPS when the sun goes down**. The Night is for Doin' Dirt; from working **Late Nights** to the more socially acceptable Criminal Enterprises: *always **AFTER*** the sun dips below the horizon. At which time it is perfectly acceptable to meet your secret lover; Afternoon Delights happen, though there is greater potential for discovery. Keeping Secrets isn't **done** in Necropolis; Snitching is considered a God-given Right, which may explain the Gossip Circles and their tendency to prefer Church grounds and functions for their gatherings.

Tonight is no different; I watch a patrol cruiser pull up in front of a house where I know a stripper lives. If anyone happens to check the log books they'll find it was scheduled for a Show of Force park-job in that neighborhood. So on the surface its placement is legit; what doesn't show up is the Assassin taking his share of the stripper's money along with getting his rocks off. She doesn't like having three Pimps (the strip club owner, her boyfriend *and* the Assassin) but it has some privileges; two blocks away a Judge takes his pleasure from a single mother with a serious coke habit and a few low-end connections who benefit from her pillow talk. Not far from this a black female Assassin drives aimlessly, trying to figure out if she can safely go to Internal Affairs about the sexual harassment she experienced. She's a local female and knows her so-called brethren will quickly forget she's one of them, *remember* she's black and suddenly she's faced with more nightmares than her roughest encounter with a wannabe Blood gang-banger.

If that doesn't make one feel comfortable then perhaps staring at the non-power players will help. Now remember: Necropolis does not have Big City problems; the virtual sea of Bloods is nothing more than a fashion trend, one that will fade once rap music gets away from the drug-and-violence soaked pathway which continues to make rappers rich and poison Da Hood. That the city's STD incidents is **well** above the national average means nothing; Miss Chase (three doors down from where the Judge is, mind) is *very* concerned about that statistic. Her teenage granddaughter keeps boyfriends only until her voracious sexual appetite finds someone with a paycheck large enough to compensate for her reckless spending. Around the corner from the patrol car two teenagers find a dark shadow to fuck in; the guy's terrified, but not enough to figure out that fucking a **fifteen-in-ten-minutes year old** is sickening and WRONG!!! The girl just hopes he's got some killer kush, and is ready to jack his ass if he tries to Fuck-and-Flee. Occasionally a car will cruise through the Night; low music and following the speed limit doesn't always mean law-abiding Citizen. I chuckle: two competing drug dealers have shipments pass each other, their cars turning down side streets right as the Assassin/Pimp steps out into the night, plastering his professional mean-mug onto his features. He spots a car approaching, judges the speed and is in hot pursuit within seconds; both vehicles pass an SUV with semi-monster tires. It's runnin' moonshine to a few spots in the city known for the illegal liquor, and driven by a sixteen year old with no license... just a family name guaranteed to get him pinched for runnin' shine even when he's a passenger in a clean car.

And did I forget to mention the grandmother steadily getting mad because her nephew is ***charging*** her for the marijuana she smokes? It's not his fault; there **isn't** any cheap weed available in town and he doesn't have a vehicle to go out into the county, a solid two hour round-trip. If his boy's Baby Mama would calm down, **maybe** he could cut a deal there; unfortunately she's seriously heated. Her Baby Daddy (one of three, the one who actually **has** money) was seen leaving, to use her words, "... some ho's house..." by one of her close friends and she isn't buying his excuse. She should; the **only** reason he was there was to score some pain pills for a guy he knows at work. Biz... never pleasure; swapping Sex for drugs is a time-proven Trade Tactic, and with his markup she won't pay a dime to get her car fixed tomorrow... if she doesn't piss Baby Daddy off to the point where he says, "Fuck it!!" and spends the money at the poker game he left just to deal with her rant.

Should I mention the daughter trying to ignore the sex sounds coming from her mother's bedroom? I wish I could ignore her powerful Prayers to God; she doesn't want her mother to have so many boyfriends and ***begs*** God to bring her Daddy back. Innocent child, completely unaware that her father is a meth-head and abusive drunk; she doesn't know or understand that her mother whores herself out to stay off Welfare. Momma is terrified of the day when her daughter **will** understand; when she's not earning the rent and car payment she pops pills and tries to forget her abusive ex-fiancée's words: *She's gonna turn out to be just like you -* ***A COMMON SLUT AN' WHORE!!!!***

Perhaps I'll wait... until Sunday; it's the best time to see the best in people... unless you're in Necropolis. Then it becomes the best day to see the worst within a so-called Christian Soul; it starts before Bible school, the calls as church members check up on those they **know** won't be attending: easier to gossip about someone who isn't there to defend themselves. The sick and shut-in get a tacit nod at the end of service, and are promptly forgotten until afterwards when **they** are considered fair game for gossip/rumor/cruel, snide comments and jokes. Any racial bias is limited to how loud the comments are; African American churches take that crown. So the overpowering cologne and perfume stench isn't confined to one denomination or congregation, and its Reason crosses those barriers as well. Some attempt to cover up Saturday Night funk, be it alcohol, marijuana or Club/Sex stench; the ones looking to catch a Good Man/Woman are, in some respects, using their Worship Time in lieu of hitting Da Club or going to a secular social event. Then again, Good Men and Women are ***supposed*** to be pillars of the Church Community according to Christian doctrine; to use a rude phraseology: *you Hunt where there is Prey.*

And according to that same doctrine, after service: dinner with the Family; yet today's societal demands means there is little **time** for *anyone* to prepare a meal. Dinner typically means crashing a restaurant; as a professional Cook I know this pattern **VERY** well, and I've seen quite a bit. Enough to seriously question the concept of proper Christian behavior when out in Public; more often than not restaurants get *angry,* ***PISSY*** fresh-from-church patrons. As for the Family Unit, I stopped questioning its place within society long ago; families fresh from church service tend to treat Sunday Dinner at the restaurant as a way to **unwind** from listening to the Preacher/Pastor/Bishop/Reverend pontificate about this, that, and the other. I understand using Food to unwind from grinding through the work day, but to treat Sunday Service as just another work day: not so much. And I **definitely** have issues with those patrons who bring only the *worst* Human attitudes into the restaurant after sitting through Sunday service... especially those who think they have a ***RIGHT*** to treat the Servers as their personal bitch-toys, complaining about everything from the crowded conditions to the noise as children expend pent-up energy. The worst of this lot are the pure Hustlers; they do whatever possible to get their meal free, **then bitch and moan** about the service, the food, whatever. However, I do see one Street trend in this practice: *never bring Trash to the HOME!!!* So, to adhere to this unspoken rule they visit a restaurant and dump their Human garbage **there**; Sunday is a Day of Rest and one cannot Rest at Home if there are things requiring their immediate attention, such as de-stressing from being berated by the Pastor's rant on social propensities many parishioners see as *just Life*.

Necropolis likes things to fit within Social Confines; one of these irritates me to no end: their Thoughts on Restaurant Employees. Apparently you can't get and hold a **good, decent** job; after all, you work in a **RESTAURANT!!!** Only Society's Fringe Elements work there; no words can accurately describe the disdain and self-righteousness in this bullshit Logic Flow, but one word explains it, and it isn't *Respect*. **MONEY!!!!** You can't get filthy, spend-like-you-have-no-cares-or-worries rich within the restaurant industry, and Money is the **only** thing capable of gaining any Respect. Want proof? If you **OWN** a Restaurant you aren't looked at as a serious Business Person... unless you make it clear that said restaurant is a dalliance, something to waste expendable cred-flow on, and probably one of **many** such endeavors. Wondering where Sex enters this equation? **Remember those other *endeavors?!?!*** You can own a restaurant if you'd rather spend money there than on a Kept Penis/Pussy, and the restaurant may even grant you access to **temporary** penis/pussy; it **certainly** grants you access to drug dealers and users and other scum (as defined by the Genteel sleazeballs). One of the reasons a Fine Dining establishment won't succeed here is because of this stain placed on **any** restaurant; you work there because it provides a legitimate (thus: **LEGAL**) income source. By default, **you** are part of society's Fringe Elements... a Bad Seed, simply because you make your money in a restaurant; the Fine Dining label only means you have access to better quality food... *and drugs!!* Servers are there *specifically* to be insulted and shit on; Cooks should remain in the back where no one can see them. On the rare occasion where a restaurant has a Public Cooking station, only the best looking **white** males are used... to help ease the customer's mind about cleanliness and sanitation. What **really** makes this racist slant ugly is that there are African Americans who ***AGREE***.

* * * *

Like the General I was chosen for the Council because of my Empathic Power, unlike the General I'm not cagey or crafty... at least in **my** Mind. I learned how to Survive in the cracks Society does its level best to cement over or ignore, but it wasn't because of some fall from grace or a bad decision/business deal. I was born to a single mother who lived in the Projects; scuffling to survive is **NORMAL** in that environment. You learned the Hustle Game while you learned to walk, talk and piss in a toilet. You also learned other Rules, and they came in two flavors: taught by Males and taught by Females. The Rules taught by Males fixated on getting paid and laid... in that order if your instructor is a Hustler, reversed if they are Playas; you also learned to **never** trust a Female... just listen to them **occasionally** and pick out the useful information. From the Females I learned How to be a Bitch; I know that statement offends, and it should.

I was taught Respect through Fear; most kids growing up in the Projects were taught that way, and it is only now that Society is **slowly** figuring out how screwed up that methodology is... and its rather disturbing consequences. Back then, I was victim of this grand tradition: *it worked for me and **I** turned out alright!!!* I can recall happy memories, but few of them occur within the place I lived, and **fewer still** include my mother. If I want childhood **Fear** she looms large: a dark shadow ready to slap the ever-lovin' *shit* out of me for any and all *Excuses*; I couldn't please her even if Jesus **and** God showed themselves and blessed me before her eyes. Happiness, as far as my Memory goes, occurred outside of my House; my fondest memories all center around the Outside World, the odd collection of friends I obtained there and the Adventures present around every corner. Yet I remember being told constantly by every Female: *there ain't nothin' Good out there*. Between that and the Fear-Equals-Respect constantly drilled into me by harsh words and a quick slap/beating, I was **taught** to be little more than a cowering, simpering thing. All while being told that my natural intelligence was a Good Thing and to never squander it; so I guess the constant contradictions poured into my young Mind reinforced my Emapthic nature. You got good at Hearing the Meaning behind every word spoken or you got used to being slapped around. However, according to Street Law, adherence to these teachings **makes a Male into a *BITCH!!!***

All I know is this: those Lessons taught me to be constantly aware of not only my actions, but to ***expect*** them to not meet my Mothers or **any** Female's standards or approval. It was Survival Training in Da Hood, and considering I'm still alive to craft these words the **assumption** is that they were effective; this might be true, but it comes at a very heavy Price. I never learned how to react to what many African American Females consider normal social interaction, what I call Crab Attitude. I taught myself to never take anyone or anything at face value. I scrutinized every word, turned over every piece of advice, command and tidbit of information constantly until I not only understood its deeper meaning, but knew how it fit into the whole picture of my continued survival. More importantly, **I never learned how to *LIVE...***; I know how to **Survive** no matter what Life throws at me. Don't have Love? No worries; Grind hard and you'll Survive. Don't worry about having a shoulder to cry on; eventually you'll run out of tears and be left with only Pain and Suffering. Choke that shit down and take one more breath as you dig your fingers into the ground and drag your sorry ass back to your feet. I was Raised in these Streets and schooled in The Grind even inside the **House**; ***HOME*** was... and still is... a Dream and blatant Fantasy, one I'll never know as Reality.

* * * *

"Hello!" I didn't reply. Two cars, each with two Assassins; I didn't have any warrants out, so this unexpected visit from the Police was either Shake-A-Nigga-Down or they want information. Being white didn't protect me at all and I knew it; they were expecting trouble. I nodded once before taking another sip from my coffee mug, keeping my gaze moving from face to face.

"Are you Silas Quick?" The fake smile he wore evaporated as I tilted my head slightly to my left. Two took up positions perfect for checking sides and back of the house; Speaker's partner played Tough Guy Bodyguard, but his iron-set Mean Mug isn't Battle Tested. Running after some drug dealer who's terrified of being caught is one thing; **I** am something completely different. Not to mention the question was utterly insane; when was the last time an average height black male was ***mistaken*** for a six-foot-two white guy? The only thing Lord Quick and I share is hair color: black.

"Can't speak?" Here we go; pleasantries done-and-done, now comes the KKK-style Abuse of Civil Rights powered by unfounded Fear.

"Why are you here Assassins?" I placed the jade green and black mug beside me, moving my gaze from one to the other. The kids across the street stopped playing, eyes alert for what Experience tells them won't be pretty; I didn't worry about their parents since the curtain shielding the living room kept moving in that *no one is watching you* manner.

"**WHAT DID...**" Speaker stopped Tough Guy before screwing on Professional calm.

"We're looking for Silas Quick."

"He's not here."

"And you are...?"

"House Sitting."

"Got some ID, Mr. House Sitting?" Tough Guy *really* wanted to start shit; fine by me.

"Hands on your Weapon tell me **you** think I'm a threat to be gunned down." I smiled; it's been some time since I had any real action and these local jokes looked just foolish enough.

"Sir, we're not here to start trouble; we just wanna talk with Silas Quick." I shrugged. Speaker sighed, gearing up to be utter Asshole. The muffled roar attracted their attention; a black SUV pulled into view, stopping in the middle of the street. One glance at the ominous non-reflective black windows and slightly elevated suspension says it all: Armored Transport.

"You're blocking the driveway and keeping me from gettin' to work on time."

"Where do you work?" I smiled slowly, allowing the Killer's Glee to fill every stray nook and cranny within my body.

"Darkhaven Manor; good day." I stood.

"You weren't..." Speaker stopped Tough Guy once more; I saw his Thoughts rattle behind his dark blue eyes. They shook the Veil just enough to reveal the putrid Infestation to my Sight; I'm going to enjoy his slow, agonizing Death when I tear it from his Mind.

"You forgot your coffee mug," Speaker said. I extended my left hand slightly from my side, but I kept my pace and never looked back. Didn't need to see the shock as it rose from the wood deck, floating steadily into my fingers. However, when one of Assassins whispered, "Another one..." I took time to Mind Rape him for an explanation, leaving several blood clots to fester; they won't kill him... **yet**... but the headaches will definitely find an annoying timing: every time his beloved Wife asks him ***any*** question.

* * * *

* * * *

Assassins; looking for Quick?

Sent by his former employer no less; hope the pussy was good... may well be his last.

And you left their Minds in tact? I'm impressed.

It was difficult; I'd rather leave them brain-dead. One could use a CAT-Scan in a few days.

Good thing you didn't. We've got enough trouble without you piling up dead lawmen like firewood; happen to find out what they wanted when you Mind Raped Officer Daniels?

That would take... restraint.

I see. Ready?

They're gonna follow.

I know; that will be taken care of ***quietly****. Right now you're needed at the Manor.*

* * * *

* * * *

I didn't look at the Assassins as I slid into the armored SUV; I was more interested in Ace's funky Thought-Speak after images. I'd heard he was a Denizen, but the Feel of his Words went beyond the somewhat inhuman tone I'd encountered from other Human-shaped Denizens.

The drive wasn't long. I've seen enough back-woods wannabe-Big-Cities in the South that this one doesn't stand out. Not that I paid much attention; I was more interested in the two young men facing me. One was Summer Pale white and he didn't like me, judging from the constant sneer tugging at his upper lip; the other kept his features Samurai Peaceful. Him I know: Marcus was Meanstreak's best Pupil. I Felt his Anger simmering: a cool/hot coil working its way around his gut; from what I'd heard he was having difficulty keeping blind Rage from taking complete control over his Mind. Both wore Thoughts Consolidated security body armor beneath their black hoodies and blue jeans.

"We're here." The voice over the intercom was Ace, but it lacked the tell-tale electronic processing; briefly I wondered if it was a mistake... or just Lord Quick's trusted assistant showing off. Neither moved for several moments; then Pale Face spoke, his voice aged by his recent battles.

"Mind if I ask your name?" Pale-Face didn't bother with plastering polite over his features when he spoke; the small round black shades kept most from seeing his eyes, but did nothing to keep his growing disdain in check.

Manners; he is a Guest.

"Where's our tail?"

They stopped following our Phantom at the State Line. I nodded.

"You first, kid."

"I go by Penance." He didn't like being called a kid; I nodded slightly before turning my head towards Marcus, ignoring Penance's pissed-off posture.

"Wield the long sword broadly." Marcus narrowed his eyes, bowing less than one heartbeat later.

"Wield the companion sword closely; I've heard of you. You are called Void." I nodded. Penance didn't breathe for several seconds. Quick told me he was good. Only a natural, **powerful** Empath can penetrate my Walls; Penance Observed it quietly, Searching for either an opening or crack in its Construction.

"It is useless to scan my Thoughts; you lack true Empathic talent... and are no Killer." I exited the SUV smoothly, barely aware of the warmth suddenly radiating from my head as he tried once more to Pierce my

Thoughts. Overhead a hawk called out; I like birds of prey: efficient killers.

* * * *

* * * *

"Void?"

"Hitman from Silas' past... one of the few Puppet Masters..."

"Say again? Those guys are twisted!!! And I thought Lord Quick **hunted** Puppet Masters."

"True; Void is one of the best. Lord Meanstreak told me about him; used to be a Hound." Marcus sounded a little better, but Blacksoul's presence reverberated in his voice; it takes a barking shit load of inner strength to control an Inner Demon, and he was rising to the challenge rapidly. Almost **too** rapidly.

"Hunting down rogue Psions: figures; but since when did Silas **need** cold blooded killers to deal with his problems?" L.J. wasn't doing a good job at keeping Young Kid from his tone, but that was expected. He's eighteen and caught between Adulthood and the waning Days of Lost Innocence; to add to his growing pangs, he's got what may amount to the World on his shoulders. I'd say: he's done good to not curl up into a ball and whimper.

"Since he became one of the three Psions chosen to remain active during this crisis; the Council is highly impressed with you two and asked him to seek out others."

"So... we're officially on our own, Ace?" I chuckled.

"Funny, L.J.; you've been gathering Assets. The Horde?"

"A bunch of nerds with just enough Awareness to cause serious issues once the Mass Emergence happens." **NOW** he sounded like a young Leader; I could Feel his Thoughts turn over my mention of the pseudo-gang, adding it to the growing mass of chaotic Thoughts and Ideas slowly taking shape within his Mind.

"Which won't be long at this rate." I let them chew on that. Both were still nursing their recent battle scars... especially Marcus. "Marcus... you should get back to your girlfriend's place. L.J.: we've got local Biz to deal with."

* * * *

* * * *

Darkhaven Manor. Always figured the place to be, well, **dark!!** Passing through the foyer I entered the Main Hall. A wide staircase led to an alabaster railing and the upstairs area; though the ceiling appeared rather ordinary I knew enough about the place to Sense the illusion. I took in everything quickly, turning to my right only when I was certain the heavy black oak doors were secured behind me.

The Den area could hold a nice sized party; the sunken floor in the center looked tacky, but I've heard Ember, the former Lord of the Manor, often held dance parties here... along with Sex Parties for the town's elite if you believed the rumors. No furniture, and no apparent lighting; still... the soft blue/white glow gave the place a comfortable, if spooky, Feel. I continued straight towards the far right wall; that's where I smelled the pungent marijuana. I didn't hear the door to the office open, nor did any light shatter the glow.

I just Knew it was open; Silas wasn't wasting time. That... unnerved me.

Greetings. I froze.

I Greet the First Thought with Honor and Honesty.

No formalities; we have Need of your Skills, Void.

My meat-eyes saw only infinite darkness; my Mind Saw the fabled Throne of Bones perched upon a raised dais. Crafted from age-blackened dragon bones, the back was completely visible though there was no light source. Huge skeletal wings spread into the darkness; or, if you looked at it a certain way, the Darkness sharpened into the individual bones of each wing. Habit made me check my surroundings; I wasn't **in** the den... but standing in a long hallway that bled into the throne room. I hadn't moved; Reality moved around me. What was most disturbing was the sense I got from this display of Power:

Silas was in a hurry; this **wasn't** flashy or show boating... this was Time Pressure.

"By we you mean the Council."

"No. Plausible Deniability; you're working for Thoughts Consolidated in this matter. I need you to hunt down the person responsible for infecting Minds with this." A Greenish-purple glow slowly made its way from the front of the throne, drifting silently towards me. Even at a distance I Felt the vileness caged within the Thought Crystal; it Felt like the thing coiled inside officer Blue Eye's Mind.

"Once I've discovered the one responsible?"

"Contact me immediately; kill only if pressed, Void. I need information more than a pile of dead bodies... and Section 8 is not on our side." **THAT** was news.

"What happened there... if I may ask?"

"**THAT** happened; the Agents we've recently encountered were all infected by whatever that thing is." Not good; Government Agents infected by something a rogue Empath created.

"So the Treaty is broken?"

"Our only link with the Government **is** Section 8." Now I understood; the only other option for gathering information was Mind Raping Government officials: Senators, Congressmen and other staff members, heads of the NSA and CIA and the like. If the Treaty wasn't broken, Mind Raping the big wigs would *definitely* shatter it to all nine Hells.

"I'm gonna need a place to stay."

"Take my old home for the time being; I have need of someone there to keep an eye out on things."

"I get extra for house keeping duties," I reply, snorting a soft chuckle.

"You also get a bonus for obliterating any intruders; there's already been an attack, and I believe the local Assassins are infected as well."

"Is that what I Sensed earlier?"

"In its pure form, though calling it *alive* is akin to calling a virus alive. Be careful; whoever's behind this won't hesitate to use force... perhaps even kill."

Fine by me.

"One other thing: there's been an Emergence across the street from my house; keep an eye on him."

"Babysitting?"

"Personal paranoia; that... and there was an attack on my place. Defend it and those who Seek Solace on its grounds; you will be rewarded."

That's when I Sensed it: a presence so ancient it defied comprehension. I'd heard rumors about Silas being not quite Human, but dismissed them as bullshit spewed by people jealous of his position in the Council or the power he wielded. Maybe even a few people he'd royally fucked over along the way; I wasn't so sure now. It Felt as if I had been dismissed, but was still being scrutinized by... *a powerful and **ANCIENT** intelligence!!* I bowed, pulled myself up and took one step back; reflexes pulled by movement up short as I found myself suddenly **back** in the softly lit den area... **well away from the wall I KNEW I was not more than two feet in front of earlier!!!** And still there wasn't anything showy or dazzling in the display of power; might as well have been a stray Thought... and **THAT** made me afraid.

In my line of work you know how much things Cost; that I'd been offered a reward by such a powerful entity meant I was in **WAY** over my head. Dangerous ground.

EPILOGUE

"Report."

"The test went worse than expected; once more I must protest. Another area should be selected, one outside of the Council's reach."

"You mean outside of **Silas Quick's** command; your objection is duly noted   What of the traitor? Has he been secured?"

"Negative. I believe he will return to Washington, D.C. and..."

"Unlikely. He will head to New Orleans; there he will either hide or, more likely, seek to contact Lord Quick."

"Do we have assets in the area?"

"Several, ma'am... but they haven't checked in yet."

"Send backup; if I know Michaelson he's killed them."

* * * *

Midnight: Mid City, New Orleans; on the other side of the block there are three police cars and two SUV style vehicles, all of which are being crammed with black club goers who lingered too long after the shots were fired. I should thank the NOPD for their rapid response, but I have other things on my mind... like just what the fuck is going on; this is the third time someone from Section 8 has tried to capture me.

I'd almost convinced myself that the first attempt was strictly business-as-usual. Bringing down a Puppet Master isn't easy, and being saddled with a rookie agent only made things worse. When the rookie turned on me I wasn't expecting it, but dealt with it swiftly... if somewhat brutally; what I wasn't expecting was the Puppet Master's vehement denial in the attack: **"I have nothing to do with that... *ABOMINATION!!!*"** I was confused... especially when one of the guards suddenly dosed the Puppet Master with Mind Juice. Normally I'd never verify that a Psion was sent to holding, but when I check on this joker and was told he'd killed himself I became skeptical; then I was told to come to HQ and give a detailed report about his capture and subsequent questioning.

"We've already arranged transport for you; be ready."

That made me paranoid; I've been jerked back to HQ before, but always because there was an Emergence within a place which I'm familiar or the situation requires cooperation with local authorities, meaning the yokels need to have the Fear of Big Government crammed up their collective assholes without lube. This felt... **Felt...** different; my gut told me I wasn't even **close** to hearing the truth from HQ. So I called someone I knew and had them check on his actual arrival date.

"Sorry Michaelson; that information's classified. When are you coming by to see me anyway; you owe me lunch!" I chuckled.

"Gimme three days and I'll see; paperwork coming out my ass Kathy. Thanks for trying." And thanks for the warning; she's a dyed-in-the-wool lesbian who will only go out with me for brunch. She's also a good friend and someone I trust; so when she said I owed her **lunch** I knew I was in deep shit.

Lunch is the only meal where Sex isn't part of the deal; it's a personal joke I shared with her... **one I heard from Lord Silas Quick**.

*If Sex ain't part of the deal, **SOMEONE'S GETTING FUCKED!!!***

My transport arrived: a full tactical team!!! They were prepared for serious resistance, going so far as to have several powerful Artifacts actively scanning the Thoughtscape around where I was **supposed** to meet them. Unfortunately for them I was ready for that and left a phantom Image of me instead of actually lingering in that frozen wasteland. What happened next made my decision easy: one of the heavies activated a containment crystal; those things are just big enough to drain a **Mind** from the Thoughtscape... **usually**. This one snapped up my Thought illusion and had power to spare... enough to attract a very powerful Spirit. They weren't expecting that, and instead of banishing the angry entity... they ran: that isn't protocol.

Which brings me to my current predicament: running away from the scene of a crime, **the only white man in the area** unless you count the cops. Behind me were several local black males and one of them was Section 8; I spotted his Thought illusion without a moment to spare. I'd been so focused on finding Quick in his old stomping grounds that I almost missed the tell-tale distortion; then I saw a brief flicker as he raised his arm: an Artifact. I didn't waste time. I dropped a Thought illusion of my own, making it appear that he was raising a gun; one heartbeat later and the supremely drunk thug standing in the way pulled his hand canon from his waistband and fired. I'm too old for this shit.

Then someone grabbed my arm, amazing considering I had my shield Artifact powered up; I was trying to take a breath when my lungs stopped filling with air and bone-chilling cold replaced the swamp-humid hot semi-fluid. This only happens when I'm in the Thoughtscape and forget that it doesn't have air; I knew I was screwed... until I watched the Agent run past me.

Michaelson. Shit... I went from screwed to utterly violated; being dragged into the Thoughtscape by **MEANSTREAK** was not something I ever wanted. Nothing I had on me could stop him from killing me in ways I'd heard could make Satan repent for all sins past, present **and** future. Then I began breathing. Air... in the Thoughtscape.

"Meanstreak." Forget Tough Guy act; I was dead any number of ways if...

Something has infected the Minds of Section 8 operatives, and you have been targeted for Sanctioning.

I'm slightly taller than Meanstreak, but right then I felt like an insect caught between Death by Stomping and Death by drowning in pesticide. I had my answers... or did I.

"You contracted for the hit?"

They are using traditional methods.

Which meant as paranoid as I thought I was, I wasn't paranoid enough; I helped **CREATE** some of those methods under the pretense of *National Security*!!! Since I was still breathing, chances are I had Death's favorite Denizen watching over me. And **that** could mean only one thing: **SILAS KNEW SOMETHING.**

"Lead the way." Meanstreak nodded and I braced myself for the nauseating feelings I got whenever traveling through the Thoughtscape.

I am no amateur, Mortal; we are already here.

At least I was, and I wasn't in front of Darkhaven Manor; I'd gone from Big Easy humid to a thick forest draped in Winter's chill. And there was the distinct sensation of **literally** being turned around; I spun around, immediately startled by the log I accidentally kicked... and the soft, weathered voice.

"You always were a bit clumsy; put the log back into place Sheriff." Sheriff: only one Denizen ever called me that...

This was going to be a long, strange trip.

ABOUT THE AUTHOR

K.L. Miller was born and raised in Danville, Virginia. He considers New Orleans his adopted home and counts that fabled city as the inspiration behind his Urban Gothic stories. In his words, "The only real difference between the Big Easy and Necropolis is the mentalities; the Shadows are the same in both sprawls. That means the PEOPLE are the same." An avid reader and street philosopher, he spends many days thinking... when he's not working at his chosen profession, Culinary.

www.ingramcontent.com/pod-product-compliance
Lightning Source LLC
Chambersburg PA
CBHW062140170626
46813CB00002B/762
9780692251171